A CHRISTMAS FOR CAROLE

Penny Richards

A CHRISTMAS FOR CAROLE

First published in Silhouette Christmas Stories, 1989
Revised edition copyright © by Penny Richards/Penny Pincher Press, 2016
First Penny Pincher Press trade edition, 2016

Cover design by BookGraphics.net
Formatting by Rik – Wild Seas Press
(http://www.WildSeasPress.com)

ISBN: 978-0-9982775-0-9

The towering psychologist smiled again, but there was a considering light in his blue eyes. "I'm well aware of what babies do, Mrs. Chapman," he assured her. "And you can trust me to take good care of her. Believe me. I've had a lot of experience."

"Fine, then," she said, shrugging into her coat. "And it's Ms. Chapman."

"Ah," he said with a nod and another smile.

That particular smile grated on Carole's nerves. It seemed to say without words that with her attitude it was no wonder she was a Ms. instead of a Mrs., something that had been bothering her more and more the past year or so, even though her first marriage had ended in disaster.

In response, she produced an insolent gaze and let it roam from his feet to his gleaming silvery hair—which was a big mistake, she realized when her heart jumped into fifth gear. How could she have forgotten how broad his shoulders were? And why did he have to be so— so very male? The longing for something she couldn't quite put a name to made a bid for freedom, an attempt she squelched with a façade of sarcasm.

"It's good to know Katy will be in such good hands," she said in a brittle tone, grabbing her purse and slinging the narrow strap over her shoulder.

Very warm, very strong hands.

Her parting smile matched her tone. "Good bye, Mr. Nicholas. Meeting you has been...an experience."

The goodwill in his eyes faded and his heavy blond eyebrows met in a frown. "Whoa!" he said. "What got your panties in a wad?"

Carole gasped. *Panties in a wad,* indeed! What an exasperating man! Her angry eyes made another scathing survey of him. Defying logic, defying the orders of her head, her heart picked up its pace. She struggled and failed to find a logical reason for her antagonism.

"You...your choice of clothing is positively reprehensible," she sputtered at last.

"Well, that certainly clears things up, doesn't it?" he shot back. "Pardon me, but if I'd known my wardrobe was going to be under scrutiny, I'd have worn my tux."

PENNY RICHARDS

Penny Richards has been writing and selling romances since 1983. After taking some time away from to pursue other things on her "bucket list," she's back at the computer, writing stories with a wide array of topics from contemporary and historical inspirational romances to sweet romance and historical mystery, with a little poetry, short stories and non-fiction here and there. She writes from her home in a small rural town in Arkansas.

Stay in touch:

Website:
http://www.pennyrichardswrites.com
email: pennyrichardswrites@yahoo.com
Facebook: Penny Richards, Author
Facebook: Lilly Long
twitter: @pennyRwrites
Linked In: Penny Richards

Books by Penny Richards

Love Inspired Historical, "Wolf Creek" Series

Wolf Creek Wedding
Wolf Creek Homecoming
Wolf Creek Father
Wolf Creek Widow
Wolf Creek Wife

"Lilly Long Mystery" Series

Kensington Books

An Untimely Frost
Though This Be Madness (May, 2017)

A Christmas For Carole

Penny Pincher Press

CHAPTER ONE

Friday, November 25

Carole Chapman drew on her full-length Tibetan lamb's wool coat, locked up her men's clothing store, and hurried through the mall, dodging the hundreds of holiday shoppers who were busy substantiating the popular hype that Christmas shopping was more important than a day spent being thankful for the blessings they already had. Instead, as was becoming the new normal, many stores had abandoned the tradition of starting the season with Black Friday and opted to open at least part of Thanksgiving Day. The way the shoppers were pushing and shoving, it seemed they weren't at all thankful for what they already had. Instead, they resembled a feeding frenzy in their eagerness to get even more.

The season of miracles? Ha! Carole shook her head in disgust. The only miracle was that anyone survived it with her sanity intact. Carole's feet hurt, her May-I-help-you smile felt frozen into place, and if she heard "Santa Claus Is Coming to Town" one more time, she would scream. She tried to ignore the fact that Christmas songs would fill the airwaves for another month and focused on her immediate problem. She still had to decorate her shop, The

Ultimate Man, for the Christmas holidays.

She'd put off the dreaded task long enough. Hers was the only store in the entire mall that wasn't yet bedecked and beribboned and glittering with lights. Definitely old school, she liked celebrating one holiday at a time, which meant she didn't start seriously plugging Christmas sales until after Thanksgiving. The problem with the world was that no one took time to enjoy the moment, or in this case, each season in its turn. Instead, Valentine candy came out the day after Christmas and Christmas décor started showing up by the time school started. Sheer madness!

An obese man plowed into her in an attempt to skirt a teenage couple in the throes of a "meaningful discussion."

"Sorry," he murmured with a disgustingly cheerful smile as he backed away and started off through the throng.

Carole didn't acknowledge his apology. She was too busy reading the words on his sweatshirt: The Fat Man Is Coming.

"I hate to break it to you, sir," she mumbled at his retreating back, "but he's already here." She'd no sooner verbalized the unkind thought than she regretted it. With a remorseful shake of her head, she headed her dragging footsteps toward the mall exit, trying to block out the shoppers' cheery chaos. She really did need to work on her attitude.

Outside, she took a deep breath and tipped her head back to gaze at the night sky. It was cold and clear, and despite the lights of the businesses, the silvery stars shone like twinkling decorations against the black velvet of the winter sky.

Decorations, she thought ruefully. She needed decorations. The hobby and craft store down the way would have just what she needed, and it was only a couple of blocks away. The cold, wintery breath of the night brushed against her face, and she drew in a deep, bracing breath. Suddenly she couldn't bear the thought of getting into her car and breathing its canned heat. Not when the night was so glorious. She would walk. Never mind that no one walked anywhere anymore or that it was "dark thirty" and she might be mugged.

Carole glanced down the street. It was well lighted and busy with traffic. She glanced down at the high-heeled boots she was wearing, a not-so-subtle reminder that her feet were killing her. Still, she wanted to walk.

Hugging her coat more tightly around her, she started off across the parking lot toward the big church that was situated between the mall and the hobby store. Surely she'd be safe in this area. Besides, if a mugger even thought of accosting her, she's start singing "Santa Claus Is Coming to Town" in a loud voice. That should send him running.

Christmas. Nothing but a commercial scam designed to eke as much money as possible from unsuspecting shoppers. While she couldn't deny that the season helped her business, she personally felt it was all a travesty. People frittered away money they couldn't afford, charging their credit cards to the hilt, and then spent the rest of the year paying for one day's enjoyment.

Why not just show your loved ones some care and consideration each day of the year, instead of trying to make up for the lapses in your relationships with a single lavish display of affection?

Carole struggled to squelch the bitterness that stemmed from sixteen Christmases—sixteen years—spent in a church-affiliated children's home. Every year during the holidays the children had received gifts tagged either "Boy" or "Girl," with the appropriate age alongside. Yet, even though the gifts were plentiful and appreciated, few of those who donated them took time to come to the home to meet the nameless, faceless kids they'd shopped for.

Ah, well, what did it matter?

She crossed the side street between the mall and the church. The imposing silhouette of the building sparked a pang of guilt. She remembered almost everything at the children's home revolving around God, but since leaving there she'd let her service and her attendance fade into the past she'd tried so hard to blot out. And after her divorce from Dan, she'd felt God had really let her down. For the first time she could remember, she felt a little guilty about that. God hadn't let her down. Dan had.

Pushing aside the feeling, she forced her thoughts back to her store windows. Maybe she'd buy an assortment of glossy chartreuse green, purple and hot pink shopping bags and tissue paper and have some sweaters, ties and belts spilling over the tops. Or maybe she'd—

A soft mewling sound brought her thoughts and her steps up short. She tilted her head and listened. There it was again. A faint wailing that sounded like a baby crying. She looked across the street. Nothing there but the glass company's empty parking lot. There was no one behind her, no one ahead of her and nothing to her left but the floodlit nativity scene in front of the church. Nothing unusual. Just the manger and the standard figures of Joseph. Mary, three wise men, a couple of lambs and a donkey.

Lured by the sound, Carole started across the frosty grass toward the precious family. No doubt about it, she thought, as she stumbled over the uneven ground, the season was really getting to her. Was she actually going to look in the manger to see if there was a baby there? No doubt about it. She'd flipped. Toppled over the edge. Yet she kept walking, drawn by a force she couldn't explain. As she approached the manger, the sound grew louder.

What if the police saw her? Would she be arrested for trespassing? Disturbing a crèche? What could she say? *I'm sorry, officer, but I thought I heard a baby crying and it sounded as if it was coming from this manger?"* She shook her head and covered the last few feet to the wooden trough filled with fresh amber-hued straw.

To her utter amazement, there, wrapped in a worn blanket and waving its tiny fists, lay a real live baby. Carole stared at the child and expelled the breath she wasn't aware she'd been holding. She hadn't gone off the deep end. This was no figment of her imagination. This was real. Alarmingly real. For a moment she was too stunned to move, but she finally knelt beside the manger and looked at the child.

The infant didn't look newborn, but it wasn't very old, either. It was wearing a knitted cap that was pulled down over its ears and an outfit that covered its hands. A pacifier lay near its head, almost hidden in the folds of the blanket that had been adjusted to block the wind.

It took only a second for Carole to realize what had happened. Someone had abandoned the baby. Red-hot anger, fueled by the memory of her own similar circumstances, rushed through her. What kind of person could leave a baby outside in the winter?

Without further thought, Carole retrieved the pacifier and, careful to support the baby's head—she'd heard that somewhere—scooped the infant into her arms. She didn't know much about babies, but she knew that pacifiers were supposed to keep them from crying. She gently thrust the plastic nipple into the tiny bow-shaped mouth. Miracle of miracles, the wailing stopped.

She breathed a sigh of relief and looked toward the busy street, once more realizing that she was standing in the floodlights illuminating the nativity scene. Good grief! What would people think if they saw her standing there? Opening her coat, she tucked the baby inside. Then, holding it close against her shoulder, she started toward her car. Christmas decorations for The Ultimate Man would have to wait.

With a bouncing gait, she trekked to her car, aware of the baby's muffled sucking. She approached her little red sports car with a prayer of thanksgiving. It wouldn't take long to warm up the interior. Unlocking the door, she eased inside, turning on the ignition and setting the heater on high.

As soon as warmth began to spill from the vents, she took the baby from her shoulder and laid it on the seat. It promptly spit out the pacifier and began to cry again, its little mouth wide open and filling the car with ear-splitting wails. Carole tried to insert the pacifier again, but the baby was having no more of it.

She gnawed her bottom lip and wondered what she should do. Change its diaper? Feed it? She didn't have diapers or formula, but there was a drugstore on the corner just down the street, and ...

Get real, Carole. You can't just keep it. What are you going to do?

The seriousness of the situation struck her. She didn't know how to take care of a baby. She was a thirty-year-old businesswoman who knew more about fashion merchandising and changing window displays than she did about buying formula and changing diapers.

The baby had been abandoned—a situation the police should look into. But the thought of taking the baby to the police station was unbearable. What did a bunch of blue-uniformed men know about taking care of a baby? Probably even less than she did. She tried again to get the baby to take the pacifier.

"Please, God," she said frantically, closing her eyes and resting her cheek on her arms that were crossed on the steering wheel. "Help me."

Even as she muttered the little prayer, she was struck by the realization that it was the first time she had called on the Lord for anything since... Shame suffused her for the second time that evening. She couldn't recall the last time she'd talked to God. The baby gave another full-throated scream, and Carole opened her eyes. To her surprise, her gaze landed on a billboard on the corner. For as long as she could remember, the huge sign had advertised the medical center a few blocks away. She blinked in surprise at the rightness of it.

Of course! The hospital was nearby and the baby should probably get medical attention. God alone knew how long it had been exposed to the cold night air or when it had been fed last. Carole buckled up, put the car into gear and started out of the parking lot. Why hadn't she thought of it sooner?

An hour later, Carole wasn't sure the hospital had been such a good idea after all. The baby had been whisked away into some inner sanctum, and a pediatrician had been called. She'd thought she'd drop off the infant and be free to go, but instead, the hospital had called the police station and insisted that she stay until the officers arrived to ask her some questions.

Which they'd been doing for the past hour.

"Are we finished, Officer Gibson?" she asked the heavyset, balding man who had been taking notes while, while from the looks of things, his younger partner flirted with the pretty young woman at the emergency room desk. "I'd like to find out how the baby is doing and go home. It's been quite a day."

The officer looked up with a tired expression of his own. "We're almost finished."

Carole barely heard. Her attention was on the younger officer who'd just answered a summons from a nearby doorway. "Fine," she said, reaching for her coat and designer purse. "But I really can't think of anything else to tell you."

"Is it yours?"

Stunned by the question, Carole turned with a frown. "I beg your pardon?"

"Is the baby yours?"

"Mine?" she said with a wry twist of her lips. She held up her left hand and waggled her fingers, indicating the bare ring finger. "I'm not even married."

He shrugged. "All the more reason to dump a kid."

Carole counted to ten and let that soak in. Having been "dumped" herself, abandoning a child wasn't an option she would ever consider, married or not. She tried to control her rising temper. "It's not my baby," she told him, enunciating carefully. "Why would you even think it was?"

"Happens pretty often. A few months ago, someone left a baby right here on the hospital steps. A couple of bystanders said they saw a woman hanging around outside until someone noticed the kid and took it inside."

"I fail to see the connection," Carole told him in a frosty voice.

The policeman met her gaze head on. "It seems pretty plain to me. Sometimes even though a mother is abandoning a child, she wants to stick around to make certain it's being taken care of. It crossed my mind that maybe that's why you brought the baby in. Maybe you concocted the whole story about finding it and maybe you're sticking around to see what's going to happen. Just to be on the safe side."

Carole shook her head, her glossy brown hair brushing her cheeks. "You're wrong, Officer. I'm 'sticking around' because no one will let me go home."

"Hey, Al!" the young officer called as he came back through the doorway. "Come look at this."

Al Gibson rose and crossed the room. Seeing that the other policeman held the baby's blanket and a plastic bag from a local grocery store, Carole joined him.

"What is it?" she asked, regarding the bag.

"A few baby things that were wrapped up with her. They're worn out but clean. There was a bottle of water, too."

Of everything the policeman had said, only one thing registered.

"Her?" Carole echoed, "It's a girl?"

The young officer smiled. "Yeah. A girl named Katy. The mother left a note inside the blanket. Said she had four other kids. Her old man skipped out on her, her milk dried up, and she can't take care of this baby. She said God told her where to leave Katy. That He'd see to it she was found."

"What a fruitcake," Al Gibson said with a shake of his head.

Carole barely noticed. She was too busy remembering the unusual set of circumstances that had led her to the baby. Since when had she walked anywhere when she could drive? And why had she chosen to walk tonight when she was so tired and out of sorts? A faint, sick feeling swept through her. If she'd chosen to drive, how long might it have been before someone came along and found Katy? Would she have been found before she...

"How is she?" Carole blurted, refusing to entertain the notion of what might have happened if she *hadn't* come along.

"Fine. Doc says she's a couple of months old. Healthy. Apparently she hadn't been out there too long. She was wrapped up good, but she was one hungry little girl."

Relief made Carole weak. She managed a slight smile. Maybe there really were guardian angels.

"You can go now, if you like, Ms. Chapman," Officer Gibson said kindly. "If we need you, we'll give you a call."

Carole nodded, suddenly very tired. "What's going to happen to...Katy?"

"They've already called Chris to come pick her up," the older officer said.

"Chris?"

Al Gibson nodded. "Chris Nicholas. The police psychologist."

Chris Nicholas. A psychologist. A feeling of relief swept through Carole. A woman like that should be a safe bet to provide a good, stable environment for a baby, she thought.

"Chris is an approved foster parent who can pick up a child on short notice when we need to get one out of a bad situation," the officer explained. "He'll keep Katy until we find her mother, or a permanent foster home."

"*He?*" Carole echoed in disbelief. But even as the shock began to take hold, a reassuring thought occurred to her. "There *is* a Mrs. Nicholas, isn't there?"

Officer Gibson shook his head. "No. But don't worry. Chris is well-qualified. He's a widower with three kids of his own."

Before Carole had a chance to digest this new information, Al gestured toward the emergency room entrance. An aged pickup covered with a film of red Louisiana dust and sporting a dented right fender pulled to a screeching stop. Carole's eyes widened and her heart sank as a veritable giant of a man unfolded his length from the disreputable truck's interior.

Chris Nicholas must have stood six-foot-four and was so broad through the shoulders that he looked as if he were wearing football gear. His hair, which was way past needing cutting, was so blonde it was almost white, which contrasted sharply with the stubble shadowing his cheeks. Not a beard, really. More like he hadn't taken time to shave for a couple of days.

But that wasn't the worst of it, she realized as her horrified, style-conscious gaze roamed from the top of his head to his large feet. If clothes made the man as the fashion industry was fond of proclaiming, this specimen of masculinity was in deep trouble. You couldn't get any farther from the "ultimate man" if you tried.

He was wearing faded, ragged jeans with a hole in the thigh. His sneakers, which sported a familiar logo and had seen better days, were worn without socks. Appalled, she shifted her gaze upward. Though it was hard to believe it was possible, things got worse. A faded, plaid shirt in an unlikely combination of orange, black and teal had been pulled on over a thermal undershirt and thrust haphazardly into the waistband of the dreadful jeans. The sleeves were rolled to the elbow, exposing powerful looking forearms covered with a dusting of fair hair. Instead of a coat, he wore only a tan down vest.

What was going on? she wondered in amazement. Shouldn't a psychologist dress the part? Shouldn't he look like the professional he was supposed to be? How could this...this man who looked like a street person be qualified as a foster parent, much less a psychologist?

CHAPTER TWO

How on earth could she let this man take Katy home with him?

"Hey, Chris," the younger policeman said, holding out his hand. "Good to see you."

The newcomer shook hands with both officers. "You too. How's the baby?"

"Doc says she's great. They're gathering up some formula and stuff for you."

"Good."

Al Gibson gestured toward Carole. "This is Carole Chapman. She found Katy in the manger in front of the Baptist church."

The police psychologist turned, his hand extended and the corners of his mouth lifting in an easy, incredibly sweet smile. "Hello Carole Chapman. I'm Chris Nicholas."

Ingrained politeness made her offer her own hand, but manners had nothing to do with her reaction. The warmth of his smile and the heat and strength of his fingers as they wrapped around hers caused Carole to forget that he was dressed as a Paul Bunyan look-alike. For the first time in a long time she was very much aware that she was a woman, a single woman who...

...who was perfectly happy with her marital status!

The sudden, unfamiliar and unwanted

awareness sent a jolt of anger through her. Hadn't she learned her lesson about men when Dan walked away after two short years of marriage? Still, style or lack of it, one thing was certain. There was no denying that everything about the police psychologist screamed "male." Carole gave a little shiver that had nothing to do with the draft of cold air accompanying the giant through the door.

She gathered her wayward thoughts and mustered the professional manner that had seen her though so many rough patches the past few years. She even managed a barely audible "Hello."

"You found Katy in front of the church by the mall?" he asked.

"Yes," she said, pulling her hand free of his grip. She didn't like the breathless feeling she experienced when he touched her. Besides, she was tired of answering questions. She just wanted to make certain the baby was in good hands so she could go home to a hot bath and a warm bed.

"Look, are you sure you can take care of a baby?" she queried, using the question as a defense against her befuddled emotions. "I mean, we aren't talking about a puppy here. She's going to cry during the night and need her diapers changed, and—"

The towering psychologist smiled again, but there was a considering light in his blue eyes. "I'm well aware of what babies do, Mrs. Chapman," he assured her. "And you can trust me to take good care of her. Believe me. I've had a lot of experience."

"Fine, then," she said, shrugging into her coat. "And it's Ms. Chapman."

"Ah," he said with a nod and another smile.

That particular smile grated on Carole's nerves. It seemed to say without words that with her attitude it was no wonder she was a Ms. instead of a Mrs., something that had been bothering her more and more the past year or so, even though her first marriage *had* ended in disaster.

In response, she produced an insolent gaze and let it roam from his feet to his gleaming silvery hair—which was a big mistake, she realized when her heart jumped into fifth gear. How could she have forgotten how broad his shoulders were? And why did he have to be so—so very male? The longing for something she couldn't quite put a name to made a bid for freedom, an attempt she squelched with a façade of sarcasm.

"It's good to know Katy will be in such good hands," she said in a brittle tone, grabbing her purse and slinging the narrow strap over her shoulder.

Very warm, very strong hands.

Her parting smile matched her tone. "Good bye, Mr. Nicholas. Meeting you has been...an experience."

The goodwill in his eyes faded and his heavy blond eyebrows met in a frown. "Whoa!" he said. "What got your panties in a wad?"

Carole gasped. *Panties in a wad,* indeed! What an uncouth man! Her angry eyes made another scathing survey of him. Defying logic, defying the orders of her head, her heart picked up its pace. She struggled and failed to find a logical reason for her antagonism.

"You...your choice of clothing is positively reprehensible," she sputtered at last.

"Well, that certainly clears things up, doesn't it?" he shot back. "Pardon me, but if I'd known my wardrobe was going to be under scrutiny, I'd have worn my tux."

Vivid blue eyes locked with deep brown. Al Gibson and his partner looked on in astonishment.

Shame coursed through Chris. It wasn't like him to lose his calm, but then, people weren't usually so critical. Of course, he wasn't in the habit of meeting folks in his everyday duds unless they visited the farm, either.

As he stood staring into her eyes and thought about the situation, Chris saw Carole Chapman's gaze waver. He could almost see her mentally backing down. Was that a glimmer of pain in her eyes? Why? The male part of him, the part of him that thought she was the most stunning woman he'd seen in ages, stepped aside for the psychologist part of him.

"Look," he said, suddenly all therapist. "I'm sorry if we got off on the wrong foot. I apologize. You're right. I'm not exactly dressed to impress, but I was cleaning the barn when the hospital called."

His sudden contrition took Carole by surprise. She took a calming breath. He'd been cleaning the barn. Maybe she'd judged him too harshly. Despite the shivery feelings he inspired in her and the fact that he had horrendous taste in clothing, any man who took in children had to be a good person, didn't he?

She sighed and shook her head. "No, it was my fault," she countered. "It's been a long day, and I'm tired. Chalk it up to bad manners and exhaustion."

"Here she is!" The cheery words preceded the blue-scrub-clad nurse who cradled a small bundle against her ample bosom. She held her little burden out to Chris, who grinned and said, "'Lo, Margaret."

"Hi there, handsome," the middle-aged nurse replied, transferring Katy into his waiting arms. "You got yourself a real beauty this time."

The corners of Chris's mouth lifted in another smile. "Let's see." He pulled the blanket away from the baby's face. "Oh, wow! She is pretty, isn't she?"

He glanced over at Carole. "Want to take a last look?"

Without answering, Carole closed the few feet separating them and, sidling nearer, peeked at the baby. The infant was sleeping, her fair lashes fanning out over her sleep-pink cheeks. A rush of something, an unlikely combination of sorrow and deep longing washed through her, and she felt the prickling of tears behind her eyelids. How could anyone just leave the life and fate of a baby to the care—or abuse—of strangers and the elements?

Blinking back the threatening moisture and avoiding eye contact with the man standing next to her, she stepped away and said, "I'm sure you'll take excellent care of her."

She wondered if the others heard the emotion in her voice and wondered again why the situation was having such an impact on her. She shot a quick glance at Chris, who said, "I'll do my best."

Carole glanced away and nodded, heading her steps for the exit before she lost her tenuous control of her tears.

Saturday, November 26

If possible, Saturday's shoppers seemed as eager to get on with their holiday purchasing as Friday's had been. Carole assigned her two helpers to dealing with the customers while she set about transforming the store from autumn to the magic of the Christmas season.

Strangely, the task wasn't as bad as she'd expected, maybe because her mind wasn't really on decorating. Instead, her thoughts were filled with Katy and the woman who'd left her behind. If she were honest, she'd admit that there was even the occasional, random thought that centered on the good-looking psychologist.

Those she tried to ignore.

She thought about the note that was found

with the baby. Maybe she'd judged Katy's mom too harshly. It appeared the woman was trying to give her daughter a chance at a better life. Still, Carole shuddered to think what might have happened if she hadn't found Katy when she did. Instead of the happy ending it was, the situation had possessed all the elements of a potential tragedy. Carole couldn't help wondering what would happen to Katy now. Would she be placed in a home or a series of foster homes the way Carole had been?

As she contemplated foster homes, her thoughts turned automatically to Chris. How long would Katy be allowed to stay with him? And more to the point, how was she doing in his care? Reason told Carole that the psychologist must be more than competent to be called on such short notice the way he had been. Nevertheless, she'd still like to see for herself how Katy was faring.

Carole fluffed a sheet of red tissue paper and shook her head. Checking on Katy would mean facing Chris Nicholas again. She wasn't sure that would be wise, especially when her heart took a nosedive at the prospect of seeing him again. Resolutely, she pushed the notion out of her head. She didn't have time for checking on babies or ridiculously handsome men. She had a store to manage.

Still, when she crawled into her solitary bed that night, her last thought was of Chris Nicholas's warm, friendly smile....

Sunday, November 27

Carole was than thankful that it was her assistant manager's Sunday to work. More than ready for a break from the madness of the mall, the prospect of cleaning her apartment had been a welcome task, and things were soon clean and orderly once more. By midafternoon, she found herself staring out the window, sipping a cup of gourmet hot chocolate and thinking of Katy again. On impulse, she looked up the number of the police station on her cell phone and asked to speak to Officer Al Gibson.

"Gibson," came his scratchy, familiar voice a few moments later.

"Officer Gibson, this is Carole Chapman. I'm the one who found Katy the other night," she said without preamble.

"Oh, right!" he said. "How's it going, Ms. Chapman?"

"Fine." She paused. "I was wondering if you've heard how Katy is doing."

"I can't say that I have. Once they've been turned over to foster care, that's it for us, and I haven't run into Chris since the other night."

"Oh."

"If you're worried about her, why don't you run on out and check on her yourself," the policeman suggested. "Chris won't mind."

The thought of making a trip to Chris Nicholas's house left her breathless, even though a secret part of her heart whispered that Al Gibson's suggestion was only corroborating her own yearning to do just that. She had no idea what was happening to her, but for some reason, her heart had been overriding her brain the past few days, longing winning out over common sense.

"Oh, I don't know..."

"Let me give you his address," Gibson offered. "Just in case."

Thirty minutes later, Carole was pulling into the driveway of Chris Nicholas's farm. The house, a Cajun-style cedar with a porch across the front, was set in the midst of a small pecan grove. The naked branches of the trees stood starkly beautiful against the gray winter sky. Beyond the trees and a barn stretched acres of pastureland, brown now with dead grass. Several head of beef cattle munched on large rolls of hay, and half-a-dozen—no, seven, she counted—swans swam majestically across the smooth surface of a large pond. A flock of noisy ducks paddled along beside them.

The barn looked freshly painted, and the fence stood straight and taut. It looked like something from a Currier and Ives painting. Carole imagined that the scene before her would be even more spectacular in the springtime, with green grass undulating in a soft breeze. Reluctantly, she conceded that it was the perfect environment for growing children. And, unlike its owner, the farm was well- tended.

Wrapped in surprising satisfaction, she got out of the car and breathed in a deep draft of the crisp air that held the merest hint of wood smoke. Though the temperatures had gone down to freezing the night before, in typical Louisiana fashion, the winter sunshine had sent the mercury soaring into the low sixties as the day progressed. It was a perfect afternoon for a country outing. The melancholy sound of two turtledoves calling to each other evoked a sudden surge of uncertainly. Had she done the right thing by coming?

Lost in thought, she watched a trio of colorful, exotic-looking hens parade across the drive, followed by a cocky rooster who was doing his best to keep them in line. Smiling at his nervous antics, Carole was once more propelled into action. She rounded the hood of her car and started for the front door.

A sudden honking and hissing assailed her ears. She stopped dead in her tracks. Almost simultaneously, an earsplitting yell escaped the interior of the house. Carole's confused, wide-eyed gaze darted from the house to the six geese approaching her at a dead run, their wings outspread, their intent clear: *Stop the intruder!*

Instinct sent her racing back to the car. As she attempted an Olympics-style leap to the hood, the front door of the house burst open and a teenage boy flung himself off the porch waving his arms like a mad man. "Go on!" he yelled. "Get out of here!"

CHAPTER THREE

Carole stared at the irate teen, unable to believe he was running her off the place so venomously. She supposed she should have called first, but until she'd found herself punching in the address on her phone, she wasn't aware she'd made the decision to check on the baby.

"I'm sor—"

"Get out of here you miserable pack of pillow stuffing!" the young man shouted, interrupting her faltering apology.

Understanding replaced her fear and relief flooded her. He wasn't talking to her at all! He was yelling at the gaggle of geese.

At the sound of his voice, or perhaps it was the waving of his arms, the geese stopped honking, turned, and ambled away.

Drawing a shaky breath, she eased her boot-clad feet to the ground and prayed her trembling legs would hold her. She'd heard that geese made good watch dogs but had never seen them in action before.

"Sorry about that," the young man said with a wry smile, raking a hand through his short dark hair. "Unfortunately the geese are a lot better at announcing strangers than Shep is."

He gestured toward a Catahoula hog dog sleeping in a once-glorious bed of yellow and rust-hued mums. In recognition of his name, the dog lifted his head, yawned and slapped his tail against the ground a couple of times.

Carole couldn't help smiling. "Shep looks like a ball of fire all right," she said.

The boy smiled in return. "I'm Brian Nicholas. Can I help you with something?"

Before Carole could do more than register the fact that he must be Chris's son, a gravelly voice that was like fingernails scraping on a chalkboard wafted through the door that still stood ajar. "There's one!"

Seeing the look on her face, Brian grinned. "It's okay. That's only Sebastian."

"Sebastian?"

"Our parrot. Everyone's trying to round up the lords."

"Oh." For some reason, Brian seemed to think his explanation cleared matters up, but Carole was as in the dark as ever about what was going on inside the Nicholas house. What or who were the 'lords', what had they escaped and how on earth did you round them up?

Then, realizing that Brian was staring at her, waiting for an explanation of why she was there, she said, "I'm Carole Chapman. I found Katy at the church the other night. I just wanted to see how things were going."

Brian nodded. "Oh, yeah. Dad told us all about you. Katy's fine. It's kinda wild in there right now, but come on in and see for yourself," he offered, starting toward the wide porch steps.

"I don't want to intrude," she said. "This sounds like a bad time."

"Probably as good as it gets," Brian tossed over his shoulder.

Wild hardly did justice to the scene that greeted Carole when she stepped into the spacious living area. Bedlam might be a better description. What calm remained after her encounter with the geese fled as she scanned the cluttered room and tried to figure out what was going on. There was so much confusion it was a little hard to piece things together.

Three boys of various sizes and descriptions, a little blonde girl and a second dog, which looked like a dirty mop, scrambled over the floor and under tables in pursuit of something that Carole supposed were the fugitive lords. A pretty teenage girl sat on the back of the sofa holding a bottle of nail polish out of harm's way. A huge Amazon parrot sat in the upper branches of a lemon tree, keeping out a keen eye on the goings-on.

"There's another one!"

Carole glanced toward the parrot, which was repeating its announcement, and caught sight of Chris standing across the room, pointing to a chair and holding Katy, who was screaming at the top of her lungs. There was so much chaos in the room that he had no idea Carole was on the premises.

Without warning, something green leaped toward the girl on the sofa, who squealed and screamed, "Tad Nicholas, I'm going to kill you if I mess up my manicure."

The tow-haired boy lunged forward and made a wild grab.

A frog, Carole thought, slightly dazed. They were trying to catch *frogs*.

"Yeah? You and what army?" he taunted, shaking his captive in the girl's face.

The mutinous act elicited another panicked yell from the teenager and a booming "Tad!" from Chris and Sebastian.

"How many is that, Jake?" Chris asked a teenage boy holding a big glass jar.

"Ten," Jake replied as Tad added his frog to the collection. "One to go."

"Chris," Brian said, taking advantage of the relative quiet. "Ms. Chapman is here."

But Chris didn't hear. A chorus of cuckoos had begun to chime out the hour. Looking around in astonishment, Carole counted no fewer than four cuckoo clocks in the room.

"Chris!" Brian yelled, struggling to be heard over the cuckoos and the barking dog, which had just spied Carole and obviously mistaken her expensive coat for some sort of critter. Yapping with all the fury and ferocity that only small dogs seem to manage, it attacked the hem of her coat, planted its feet apart and pulled, shaking its head back and forth and snarling with the viciousness of a much larger canine.

Diverted from wondering why Brian called his father Chris, and almost in a state of shock, Carole bent over and tried to free her coat—her ridiculously expensive lamb's wool coat—when yet another frog appeared out of nowhere, leaping toward her face with a deep, throaty *rrribbitt*.

Carole jumped and shrieked.

Yelping in surprise, the dog released its hold and scrambled across the room to leap onto a chair piled with what appeared to be clean laundry. She didn't know if it was due to the unfamiliar sound of her voice in the melee or the fact that, after announcing the time, the four calling birds retired to their respective abodes, but the room grew quiet suddenly.

Feeling like an alien in an alternate universe, her gaze found Chris's. He was looking at her in surprise, as were the children. Even Katy had stopped crying.

"I got it," another youngster said, breaking the relative silence. He held the last frog aloft in both hands, a wide smile crinkling the corners of his almond-shaped eyes.

"Way to go, Mikey," Chris said, shifting his attention from Carole to the boy. Then he turned to the one she recognized as Tad who, Carole deduced, must actually be Chris's son, if the name and the hair were anything to go by.

"Get those frogs back in their aquarium, and don't let them out again, do you hear me?"

"I didn't do it!" Tad objected. "Tina dropped the picnic basket."

Chris closed his eyes. Carole wondered if he were counting to ten. "I'm almost afraid to ask," he said in a patient voice that he was apparently struggling to maintain, "but what were they doing in a picnic basket?"

"She was taking them for a walk."

"A walk?"

"Yeah. She said they must be tired of being cooped up all the time."

"Go to your room, Tad," his father said in a weary voice.

"And clean it while you're in there," Brian added.

"You wish," Tad said with true brotherly disdain. He jerked his head toward Carole. "Who's she?"

"Stop staring, Tad," the girl on the couch commanded, sliding back onto the cushions. "That's rude."

"This is Ms. Chapman," Brian announced once more. "She found Katy."

Before anyone, including Chris, could reply, Brian asked, "Would you like to sit down?" He glanced at the nearest chair where the dog was ensconced, and blushed before shooing the pup off the pile of clothes waiting to be folded and scooping them up in his arms.

"Thank you." Carole, whose legs were still trembling from her encounter with the geese and her scare with the frog, was grateful for the chance to sit and sank into the chair. She glanced at Chris, who shifted Katy to his other shoulder and gave her back a soothing pat.

"I'm sorry about the confusion," he said with a rueful smile. "Please don't think it's always like this around here."

"I understand," Carole hastened to assure him. After all, it wasn't every day that frogs were unleashed on an unsuspecting household.

"Sometimes it's worse," he told her, his expression deadpan. Then she saw that his bright blue eyes were alight with mirth. "I just wanted to give you fair warning."

"Oh," was all she could think of to say.

"So, Carole Chapman, what can I do for you?"

She met his questioning gaze and felt her face flush with heat. "It was such a pretty day that I...I thought a drive would be nice, and I—"

"You wondered how Katy was doing."

"Well, yes," she confessed, embarrassed because her motives were so obvious.

"She's doing fine." He squatted beside the chair and turned Katy so that Carole could see for herself. At that moment, Carole didn't care about Katy. She was too busy trying to place the deliciously masculine scent that radiated from him and set her heart to racing.

"Well?" he prompted, turning his head to look into her eyes.

Carole drew in a shaky breath and forced her gaze to the baby. Katy's eyes were open and tears sparkled on her dark eyelashes. Her soft hair was brushed to the side. She looked well-fed and not the least bit sleepy. She smelled nice and clean, just as a baby should smell.

Smiling, Carole looked back at Chris. Was he closer than before? His shoulders were so broad, she thought as her gaze traveled up over his square chin and the tempting curve of his upper lip.

She'd never been kissed by anyone with a beard before, not even scruffy facial hair like Chris's. Her gaze shifted to his eyes which were smiling into hers. Stylish or not, the man was definitely gorgeous and would be no matter what he wore.

"Well?"

She licked her dry lips and struggled to draw a decent breath. "She looks...fine."

"She is fine. Actually, Katy has adapted very well. Insanity must run in her family, too."

When Carole's eyes widened, so did Chris's smile.

"Let me introduce you to the troops," he said, standing and giving her some breathing room. "You've obviously met Brian. He's a senior this year."

Glad for the reprieve from Chris's disturbing nearness, Carole nodded. "Brian saved me from the geese."

"Brian is my oldest. He's been a Nicholas for about six months now."

Carole wondered if her surprise showed. It was hard to believe that Chris had bothered to adopt a boy Brian's age, since he would soon be graduating and out on his own.

"The one over there who's afraid her manicure will get messed up is my daughter, Lisa, who is in the tenth grade."

Pretty blond-haired Lisa wrinkled her nose at her father, but there was a familiar glint of mischief in her blue eyes, too. "Hello, Ms. Chapman."

Chris pointed to the boy holding the glass jar. "Jake Arnold, keeper of the frogs, also known as the lords, has only been with us since school started. He's thirteen."

Jake ducked his head shyly. "Hi."

"I don't understand," Carole confessed. "Why do you call them the "lords?""

Chris chucked. If possible the sound was even more attractive than his smile. "I'm not sure where the idea came from but they're all named after lords. You know, Lord Byron, Lord—"

"I get the picture," Carole said.

Chris reached out and riffled the hair of the smiling boy with the Oriental look. This is Mike. He's ten and I'm trying to adopt him."

Mike offered Carole a bright-eyed smile. "Yeah!"

Now that she'd had time to get a better look at the child, Carole could see that Mike had the look of a child with Down syndrome. Just for a moment her heart ached in pity, but with Mike's smile rivaling the afternoon sunshine streaming through the windows, the feeling, which she knew was misplaced, vanished.

Pointing at the thin boy with thick glasses and the blond culprit who owned the frogs, Chris said, "This is the Terrible Twosome. Tad is my own offspring. He's seven. And the eight-year-old boy genius is David Carter, who has all the makings of a computer whiz. What one of them doesn't think to get into the other one generally does."

"Me, Daddy." The prompt came from the cute little girl who was holding on to Chris's leg for dear life.

"I didn't forget you, pretty girl," Chris said, placing a big hand atop her blonde head. "This is Tina Nicholas. She three and just the tiniest bit *j-e-a-l-o-u-s* of the *b-a-b-y*." He smiled again. "And of course, you know Katy."

"Me, Daddy." The reminder came from parrot, that could obviously mimic anything he heard.

"Ah, yes," Chris said. "That noisy scoundrel is Sebastian. We're kind to kids and animals around here, even if they're ornery."

Carole thought of all the critters she'd seen outside. The Nicholas farm was quite a menagerie, both of animals and kids. The sheer number of both was overwhelming. She was filled with amazement and full of questions. For instance, where had all these kids come from, why was Chris adopting a Down syndrome child, and what had happened to his wife? But instead of asking those questions she did some quick calculating and said, "You have three biological children. Lisa, Tad and Tina, right?"

"Right," he told her with a nod. Then, changing the subject abruptly, he asked, "Would you like some coffee?"

As his warm smile had the night she'd met him, his easy offer of hospitality took Carole by surprise. "Well, I..." She hesitated, wondering if she shouldn't simply leave while she was ahead. After all, she'd seen for herself that, despite the chaos of the household, Katy was fine.

"A cup of coffee sounds wonderful," she heard herself say. "Thank you."

"Good. I think Lisa has some cookies baked." Chris turned to the roomful of children. "Get on your bedrooms, a.s.a.p. I want them clean before supper."

To Carole's surprise, the room emptied as if he'd just told them a snake had been turned loose, though she did hear some grumbling as they filed out.

"Not you, young lady," Chris said to Lisa, who was the last to leave.

Turning, she looked at him with wide-eyed innocence. "What?"

"What?" Chris echoed. He looked at Carole. "She looks smart, doesn't she? But her memory is terrible.

"Daddy!" Lisa cried.

"Sorry sweetie, but wet nails or not, it's your turn to do the kitchen."

Lisa gave him a wounded look.

"Pronto."

"But you promised you'd take me to the mall to look for a dress for the New Year's party."

"That was before we had eleven frogs escape and before company came," Chris reasoned, pointing toward the kitchen. "Go."

Lisa went. As the door swung wide, Carole glimpsed a large kitchen with dirty dishes covering every inch of counter space. She sighed in sympathy for Lisa. Past experience had taught Carole how hard it was for a girl to stand on the threshold of womanhood with no one to guide her, no one to confide in about her problems or the changes taking place in her life and her body...no one to help pick out a party dresses.

On the other hand, Lisa at least had a father who loved her and was willing to do his best at standing in for the mother who was missing in Lisa's—in all the children's—life. It had to be hard on him, trying to bring up his own family without a wife and mother. And then to take on the added responsibility of five other children...

"Hold Katy, will you?" Chris asked, the simple request breaking into the somberness of Carole's thoughts.

She looked up, her excuse already forming. She didn't want to hold Katy or to feel any more tugging on her heartstrings. "I don't—" she began, and then her gaze met his. There was a question in the clear blue depths, something that asked without words what was wrong. Carole realized suddenly that he was a very intuitive man.

He smiled at her. She wasn't certain she'd ever met a man who smiled so often, or had a smile so sweet.

"If you don't hold Katy, Lisa will have to make the coffee, and if Lisa makes the coffee, you'll never come back."

Carole wasn't even aware that she held out her arms. Without a word, Chris handed Katy over and disappeared through the swinging door that led to the kitchen. Only when he'd gone did Carole wonder why it would matter to him whether she came back or not.

CHAPTER FOUR

While Chris was in the kitchen making coffee, Carole prowled the room, rubbing Katy's back and searching for clues to what made Chris Nicholas tick while Sebastian climbed up and down the branches of the lemon tree. A huge rock fireplace with a gun cabinet built on one side dominated the room. Matching bookcases on the other side balanced the wall. A mounted deer head and a huge largemouth bass added to the rustic charm. Obviously Chris was an outdoorsman. A hunter and a fisherman. But a well-read one, she thought, eying the magazines scattered about and the titles on the book spines. Everything from the classics to John Sanford and Jeffery Deaver was represented, plus psychological journals and children's fare.

Katy began to fuss, cutting Carole's tour short. She cradled the baby in her arms and bounced her up and down a couple of times. What would she do if Katy started crying in earnest? Carole glanced toward the kitchen. How long did it take to make coffee, anyway?

She looked at the baby in her arms who gave a low, halfhearted wail and pursed her lips in a sucking motion. Was she hungry? "Oh, Katy," Carole begged. "Please don't start crying."

"What's the matter? She hungry?"

Carole looked up and saw Tad, David and Mike standing in the doorway, three small witnesses to her incompetence.

"Time Ka-dee eat?" Mike asked.

"Ka-dee eat?" Sebastian echoed.

"I don't know," Carole confessed, bouncing Katy in her arms.

"It's probably colic," David said, pushing his Coke-bottle-lens glasses farther up on his small nose. The trio sidled nearer.

"Horses get colic," Tad said in disdain.

"Tummy ache. Colic. Gas. It's all the same, Tadpole," David said with supreme confidence.

"It's all the same, Tadpole," Sebastian echoed.

"Stop calling me Tadpole!" Tad yelled.

"Stop acting like you know everything," David countered. He glanced at the clock. "I think she eats in a little while. Want us to go ask Chris?"

"That might be a good idea," Carole said.

David and Tad left the room, but Mike stayed behind. She watched as he went to a stack of baby paraphernalia in the corner and came back with a dispenser of baby wipes, a diaper and a pacifier, which he held up with a triumphant smile.

"Passie," he said, reaching up and poking it into Katy's little bow-shaped mouth. Katy accepted the pacifier eagerly. Her eyes closed, and the fretting stopped.

"No Cry-hing," Mike said, pleased with his solution. "I tell Chris."

As he left the room in search of Chris,

Carole's heart swelled with a strange blend of pity and joy. What a sweet child Mike was. She knew it couldn't be easy bringing up so many children, and one with any kind of disability was bound to require more work and concern. She wondered again why Chris would want to take on the responsibility of a child with such obvious limitations when there were so many healthy kids, kids like she had been, needing parents. Pain, as old as her memory, brought the sting of tears to her eyes.

She'd thought that as she grew older and came to a better understanding of people and life in general, she could grasp why no one had wanted to make her a part of their family. But she was thirty, and she still didn't understand. She remembered how she'd convinced herself on three different occasions that the family she was living with was going to adopt her.

The first time she'd been five and the couple had been young and attractive, parents any child would have been proud of. People had even commented on how much Carole resembled the woman, who was sterile and wanted a little girl. But after eight months, Marcia Bradley had sent Carole back to Fairhope, saying that her husband wasn't sure the timing was right to adopt, since his business kept him on the road so much. Besides, he really wanted Marcia to travel with him.

The second time she'd been told that the people loved her, but they really wanted a little boy. Carole couldn't remember what excuse she'd been given the third time. By then, she was twelve and convinced that something was wrong with her, otherwise, things would have turned out differently. She had loved them all and had wanted so much to be part of a family that loved her back. But it seemed that either she fell short in some way, and after those three heartbreaking experiences, she'd vowed she would never put herself in the position of being rejected again.

Growing up changed the rules. She'd been as attracted to boys as the any girl, but she soon learned that too often there were strings attached to a boyfriend. Her upbringing at the orphanage had instilled Christian morals in her, and she refused to play by anyone's rules but hers. Her solution was simple. Every time a guy tempted her or pushed her, *she* ended things. She'd heard far too many love-'em-and-leave–'em stories and was terrified that if she allowed herself to care too much, or if she gave them what they wanted, she would be rejected, just as she had in the past. It was far better if she was the one who walked away.

The plan worked just fine until Dan Forrester sauntered into her life.

She was twenty-five when he came along vowing his everlasting love. Of course, like the others, he expected her to prove her love, but Carole held out for a wedding ring.

She also held on too tight, Dan claimed. She wanted to be with him every moment. Didn't want him going places without her, didn't want him taking out-of-town business trips unless she went, too. After two years, Dan had tired of the prison she created and filed for a divorce. He remarried within months of the final decree.

Strangely, his leaving was the thing that made Carole take a hard look at herself and sent her to a counselor. She saw him for more than a year, and with his help, she came to terms with the scars her mother's abandonment had left on her. She'd learned hard lessons about being so needy and clingy, and she'd even learned that everyone needs some "me" time. Even her. Though she was still skeptical about love, she dated often. Her determination to avoid another broken heart had given her more time to devote to her business, which resulted in a growing clientele and a line of merchandise that drew businessmen from faraway Dallas, Little Rock and Houston. If her choices made her a lonely woman, they had also made her a successful one.

Most days she was content with the status quo, but there were times, like when she saw Mike's smile and held Katy in her arms or felt the warm sweetness of Chris's personality, she knew she was cheating Mother Nature. She wanted a family and love more than anything she could think of, but she was so fearful of taking another chance, which was why her unexpected attraction to Chris Nicholas was so disturbing. She was a normal, healthy woman with all the usual feelings and desires, and even if he dressed in clothes that looked as if they belonged among someone's castoffs, he was most definitely a hunk, and the woman in her responded to that elemental pull.

Maybe she'd been wrong in thinking he was a poor candidate for the ultimate man. As a matter of fact, now that she'd seen him in his element, she realized that his way of dressing fit his life-style just fine. And his rough-hewn good looks and impressive physique, combined with his gentle personality made him an impressive man.

"Coffee's ready."

The sound of Chris's voice sent her guilty gaze to his face and silenced the clamoring of her wayward thoughts.

"Good," she said, attempting to hide her feelings behind a too-bright smile.

He set two mugs on the coffee table and pulled a baby bottle from his shirt pocket. "Tad and David thought you might need this, but it looks like you have things under control."

"Thanks to Mike. He found Katy's pacifier."

"Works every time," Chris said with a grin. "Let me put her down so we can enjoy our coffee."

Carole nodded, eager to hand the baby over. Holding Katy made her nervous and brought back the feelings of inadequacy she usually managed to push aside. She held the baby out and Chris leaned over, sliding his hands over hers to support Katy's back and neck as the exchange was made. The warmth of his callused palms made her uncomfortable, as did his smile. Once again she found herself struggling to control the wild beating of her heart. What on earth was the matter with her? It wasn't as if he was the first handsome man she'd come into contact with. Good-looking guys came into the store all the time, so why did this one affect her when no one else had?

She didn't say a word as he left the room with Katy cradled close.

When he returned, she was still pondering why this particular man should stir her emotions when she'd managed to avoid that pitfall for the last three years.

"She's out like a light."

"That's good," Carole said, taking a sip of her coffee.

Chris sat down on the couch, facing her. "What's the matter?"

"What makes you think something's wrong?" she countered, amazed that he was so in tune to her in such a short time.

"It's my job to read people," he told her. "And you've been angry, suspicious and generally prickly ever since I met you at the hospital. I assure you that I'm as dependable as my practice allows, reasonably sane most days and I love these kids a lot. I'll take good care of Katy."

"I know that," Carole said, and realized as she spoke that she meant it.

"Then what is it?"

"Nothing. Everything." She shrugged. "The season, I guess."

"You talk in riddles, lady. Did anyone ever tell you that?" he asked with a shake of his shaggy head.

"The Christmas season," she said, rising and carrying her cup to the window. "It always brings back so many memories."

"Not good ones, obviously."

"No. Not good ones." She turned to look at

him. "I was raised in an orphanage and a series of foster homes too, Mr. Nicholas."

"Chris."

"Chris," she repeated obediently. His name sounded right on her lips, just as the need to open up to him felt right. Seeing the children in his home, knowing that he was so caring and giving made her old hurts and doubts shoot straight to the surface.

"Like Katy, I was abandoned," she confessed. "I was two when my mother left me on the doorsteps of Fairhope Children's Home."

"And you resent that."

Carole's laugh was short and bitter. "Wouldn't you resent knowing that someone loved you so little she could give you up without looking back?"

Chris shrugged his massive shoulders. "It there's one thing I've learned since I've been a counselor, it's that few things are that cut and dried. Maybe she did love you, but like Katy's mom didn't feel she could give you life's essentials, much less its advantages. At least at Fairhope she knew you'd have a roof over your head and get three square meals a day, even if no one was going to cuddle you at bedtime. That's a lot brighter picture than a kid being brought up on the streets."

He had a point, Carole thought. Maybe her mother's situation was like Katy's mom's. She'd never looked at it from that perspective.

"Is that why you feel she didn't love you?" he asked.

"I suppose." Her lips curved in a wry smile.

"No one has ever loved me."

"That's a pretty strong statement," he said. "What do you base it on?"

Despite telling herself she was talking too much, Carole heard herself say, "Oh, I don't know. Maybe on the fact that even though I lived with and learned to love several families no one cared enough to want to adopt me." She was unaware of how much of her pain the statement revealed.

"Adoption is a big decision, Carole. Huge," he told her. "Some fantastic foster parents don't want to make that final commitment for one reason or another. Sometimes they feel they can do more as that intermediate step between a bad situation and adoptive parents. And after a while, you realize that you can't adopt them all, so you have to choose."

"I can buy that," she said, "but how do you decide? Why did you adopt someone like Brian who's almost grown? And why Mike instead of Jake or David?"

"Those are fair questions," he said, nodding. "Like you, Brian needed to know someone loved him. He'd been through several foster families, wasn't doing well in school and stayed in trouble with the law. Nothing too terrible until he broke into the school with some other kids. That was the turning point. The police picked him up, the court sent him to me, and over a period of time, I realized that he felt like he'd fallen through the cracks. As you pointed out, he was too old to be adopted. The state was just waiting until he was of age so they could cut him loose. He was crying out for attention and love. I like to think I've given him that."

Chris *had* given him that, Carole realized. She had to swallow back the lump in her throat.

"And you're wondering why I'm trying to adopt Mike instead of a so-called normal child. The answer is easy. First of all, kids with any kind of handicap often never have a chance for adoption. Secondly, once you're around him for a little while, you'll see that Mike is a very lovable kid. I hope that by the time he's Brian's age he'll be able to function in the world at least enough to have some sort of independent life."

Carole blinked back another rush of tears. "What about the others?" she asked.

Chris's mouth curved in that gentle smile of his. "There have been a lot of others through the years. If you mean the kids I have now, well, Jake—"

He paused, and for just a second Carole saw a hint of anger in the depths of his blue eyes. "Jake's only here temporarily. He and his mother were in an abusive situation. She's in the process of getting a divorce and finding a decent job and a place for them to live. When we feel she's well enough established, he can go back to her.

David's parents were killed in a car accident," Chris continued. "He isn't eligible for adoption because he has an older sister—a career woman who doesn't want to be bothered with bringing up a child but won't relinquish her rights to him."

"That's terrible!" Carole cried.

"It is, but David is a survivor. And he's

smart."

"And how do your three kids feel about all this? Do they resent having their home invaded by strangers?"

"Not so far. Like I said, it's all they've ever known. Lisa is a typical teenager. I have to be careful about bringing in a girl she might feel is competition or a guy she'd go gaga over. Tad loves having someone to get into trouble with and Tina just goes with the flow. I guess they accept it because Valerie and I always did it."

"Valerie? Your wife?"

Chris nodded. "She died having Tina." His gaze found Carole's and he offered her a bittersweet smile. "It wasn't supposed to happen. No one dies in childbirth anymore." He stared into his coffee cup. "But she did."

"I'm sorry."

A trace of sorrow lingered in his eyes. "Yeah. So am I. Besides the void her dying created in my life, it left me in a bit of a predicament as far as bringing all these kids into the house."

"I thought single parents were pretty accepted nowadays."

"You're right about that, but I'm afraid that the older kids have to take on more than they should sometimes, since there's no Mrs. Nicholas to pick up the slack when I'm called away."

"Maybe you should marry again," Carole suggested, and then wished she'd kept her mouth shut. His marital status was none of her business.

His smile turned derisive. "It's hard to find a date—" he waved his left arm in a wide arc "—

much less a woman willing to take on all this."

Sunlight glittered off the gold watch circling his brawny wrist, obviously reminding him of the time. He made a low sound of annoyance.

"What is it?"

"I've got to get busy finding a baby-sitter."

"A baby-sitter?"

He nodded, already heading for the phone. "Tomorrow's Monday, and Mrs. Landry, who keeps Tina and whatever other preschoolers I have, called this morning and said she had the flu. I've got to round up someone else pretty quick."

He was going to leave Katy with a stranger? The thought brought an ache to Carole's heart.

"What are you doing tomorrow?" he asked out of the blue.

She looked at him in astonishment. "Working, why?"

"Can you get the day off?"

"What do you mean, can I—Oh no!" she said, seeing the contemplative gleam in his eyes. "I can't baby-sit. I have a business to run."

"Since you're the boss, you could take the day off, couldn't you? Ask someone else to come in for you?"

"No."

"Sure you can. One day."

"No."

"Come on," he wheedled. "Tina's no trouble. And you've been worried about Katy. This will give you an opportunity to see what her mother is missing. A chance for you to see that she's well taken care of, at least for a day."

"I don't know how to take care of a baby!" Carole cried, setting her mug on the coffee table with a thud. "I'm a businesswoman, remember?"

"You're a natural," he soothed. "Why, you had Katy asleep by the time I got here with her bottle. All you have to do is feed her, change her give her a bath—"

"A bath!" she exclaimed.

He shook his head. "Never mind. I'll give her a bath tonight."

"I can't."

"You can." His blue eyes cajoled. "Please."

The softly uttered plea was her undoing. She blew out a slow breath. If her uncharacteristic response to him so far was any indication, she had a feeling that Chris Nicholas could charm her into robbing a bank if that's what he wanted.

"You're a manipulator," she accused, pointing a well-manicured finger at him.

"I know," he confessed without an iota of remorse. "But when you're in my shoes, it helps."

CHAPTER FIVE

Carole called herself ten kinds of fool all the way home. Psychologist Chris Nicholas had learned his trade well, she thought as she pulled into her parking place at the apartment complex where she'd lived the past two years. He'd learned which emotional buttons to push to get people to talk and which ones to push to get them to agree to whatever he wanted. She let herself into the apartment with a sigh. That wasn't a fair accusation. Not really. She could have said no to his preposterous idea that she stay with Tina and Katy the next day. She should have. But she hadn't, and now she was worrying herself sick about how she was going to handle taking care of two little ones all day long. The prospect was terrifying.

Even though it was early, she got ready for bed, fixed a salad she didn't eat, called her assistant manager and asked if he would take care of the store again the next day, and then turned on the television only to find yet another Christmas movie taking up prime time.

Groaning, she pushed the remote control to change channels. A country singer and a high school chorus were doing a snappy rendition of "The Twelve Days of Christmas." What was the deal? she wondered grumpily. Where did all these movies come from? Were they cloning them on some Hollywood sound stage?

In the end, because she planned to do some bookkeeping anyway, she decided on Dickens's *A Christmas Carole*. Ebenezer Scrooge's dour attitude matched her mood much better than "Christmas Kisses." The title brought to mind an image of Chris giving her a Christmas kiss beneath the mistletoe.

Stop it with the crazy fantasies, Carole!

Work. She needed to think about work, *not* Chris kissing her! Still, she couldn't help wondering what the touch of his lips against hers would feel like. Almost desperately, she grabbed her laptop.

Somewhere between the ghosts of Christmas past and present, Carole yawned and thought longingly of bed. Her eyes burned, the columns of numbers were blurring, and she realized that she was dead tired. All that housework she'd done before driving out to the Nicholas place must be catching up with her. She propped her head on her hand as a picture of Chris ambled through her mind. *Go away, Chris!* Closing the laptop, she scooted down until her head rested on the throw pillow. She'd finish the paperwork in just a minute. As soon as she rested her aching eyes...

"Carole."

Chris was calling her. She forced her eyes open to familiar surroundings. Her laptop sat on the coffee table where she'd put it, and she was lying on the sofa, but... She sat up straighter and rubbed her hand over the worn, familiar fabric of the cushion. This wasn't her sofa, and this *wasn't* her house. She was at the children's home. She bolted upright and looked around. What on earth was going on?

She heard Chris call her name again.

"Chris?" she replied. "Where are you?"

"Right here."

She glanced toward the foot of the sofa and sure enough, there he stood, clad, as usual in his disreputable jeans and a garish flannel shirt. But there was a sort of glow around him that made her nervous.

"What are you doing here?" she squealed. "What am *I* doing here?"

"We're both here because I wanted to show you something about Christmas... about people."

"Sorry," she said. "I know all I want to know."

"Maybe so, but you *need* to know a few more things" He held out his hand. "Come with me."

Carole regarded him with a wary expression. "Where are we going? And why do you glow like that?"

"Just come."

For some reason, she put her hand in his, and the next thing she knew she was standing in the center of Fairhope Children's Home's recreation room. A huge tree stood in the corner with an impressive stack of presents piled around it. Mr. Nelson, the director, and Mrs. Hardy, the head housemother, were sorting the gifts into stacks.

An avalanche of memories swept over her. "What's going on?" she asked in a testy tone.

"Just watch."

"I've seen it before. It's Christmas, and they're getting ready for the kids," she observed. "So what?"

"Listen," Chris said drawing her nearer.

Carole tugged on his sleeve. "Stop!" she whispered. "They'll see us. Mrs. Hardy sees *everything*."

"They can't see us, Carole. No one can. Besides, Evelyn Hardy died two years ago."

"What?" Carole cried, amazed at the pang of sorrow that shot through her.

"Will you just shut up and listen?" he said in exasperation.

"Look at this," Tom Nelson was saying, holding up the fancy porcelain doll Carole had received on her eighth Christmas. "This is for Carole."

Evelyn Hardy clasped her hands together and beamed. "Isn't it beautiful? I know she's going to love it."

Carole cast Chris a maligned look. "The doll was from Mrs. Charmichael. She always sent big presents at Christmas, but did she ever come to see one of us during the year? Did she ever think to ask us what we wanted? No. She just went to the store every December, bought a bunch of expensive toys and figured that she was okay with God for another year."

Chris arched his fair eyebrows. "Is that why you've written God out of your life? Maybe you should be sure of the circumstances before you make rash judgments. Keep listening."

The sound of Mrs. Hardy's voice kept Carole from answering.

"I can't believe she does so much for us," the housemother said, a sorrowful expression on her pleasant features. "Especially when her medical bills are so high."

"I know," Mr. Nelson said. "She sends that check faithfully every month, even though she can't come and see how much good her money is doing."

Mrs. Hardy sighed. "It's too bad her dialysis forces her to stay so close to home.

"Dialysis?" Carole echoed, looking up at Chris.

"That's right," he said. "Mabel Charmichael was on dialysis for years, but she still called the home every year and asked Evelyn what each child wanted. How else do you think she knew you wanted that porcelain doll? Even if she couldn't visit, she tried to make your Christmases happy. And Andy Franklin, who sent the hobbyhorse lived in Tallahassee, Florida, and—"

"I get the picture," Carole interrupted with a sigh. "I judged them all wrongly."

"Not all," Chris corrected. "Some of them do just send a gift at Christmas and forget about the kids the rest of the year. Like you."

"What!" Carole pinned him with an angry look.

The ghostly Chris looked back, his eyebrows raised. "Don't you send a big check to the home every year?"

"W-well, yes, of course. It's the least I can do."

"You're right about that," he said with a wry smile. "It is the *least* you can do. When was the last time you visited?"

A sudden rush of shame swept through her. She suspected he already knew the answer to his question. She was guilty of not going back, just like so many of those she'd judged, but returning had always seemed too painful, and besides, that was a part of her life she wanted to forget. But now, at Chris's prodding, a new awareness washed through her.

"I...I—" she stammered.

"Isn't it true that the last time you were at Fairhope is when you walked out the door for good?"

"Yes, but—"

"No buts and no excuses. Facts are facts. Come on Carole. Let's go see the Bradleys...."

Carole knew she was really awake when she opened her eyes and saw the familiar furnishings of her living room. The television screen was filled with yet another of the infomercials that dominated nighttime television. She breathed a sigh of relief, even though the dream was sharply etched in her memory.

Her neck had a crick in it. Clamping her teeth onto her bottom lip and stifling a groan, she pushed herself into a sitting position, her sleepy gaze zeroing in on the large wall clock across the way. 2:04 a.m. Only four hours until she had to get up and head to Chris's.

Chris. Thoughts of him brought back her dream in full force. She remembered waking in the orphanage and seeing him as what? The ghost of Christmas past? Following the episode with Tom Nelson and Evelyn Hardy, he'd taken her to the Bradley's, the young couple Carole had hoped would adopt her. In her dream, Marcia Bradley had been packing Carole's clothes and crying. Her husband tried to console her, telling her that he loved her but that he needed her to himself, at least for a while.

Carole realized that just maybe, Marcia Bradley had loved her after all.

Finally, Chris took her back to the front door of the home once again. A teenage girl stood on the steps telling Evelyn Hardy that she'd found the little girl she was holding wandering along the sidewalk. The young woman had thrust the toddler into Evelyn's arms, saying that she must have wandered away from the home.

Evelyn explained that the dark-haired child wasn't one of theirs, and went to get Tom. When they returned, the child had been shut inside and the young woman was gone. Carole and Chris had seen her huddled beneath a big oak tree in a nearby wooded area, tears slipping down her cheeks.

That was my mother.

"Ridiculous!" Carole cried, leaping to her feet. It had only been a dream, some silly notions her mind had conjured up as a result of her talk with Chris and her weariness when she'd fallen asleep while watching *A Christmas Carol*. It meant nothing, except that her past, Christmases and all, still troubled her.

Monday, November 28

Carole arrived at the farm at exactly seven-thirty. To her surprise, Chris had already gone to work. As Brian led her to the kitchen, she told herself smugly that Chris hadn't been able to face her and had taken the coward's way out. Hearing the sounds coming from behind the closed door, she suspected she knew why.

Brian pushed the swinging door wide for Carole, who was followed by a waddling Sebastian squawking a loud, "Come on in."

The big, cheerful room was filled with noise, and confusion reigned once more.

Jake was sitting at one end of the table doing some last-minute studying, or at least trying to. Lisa, her makeup perfection, was desultorily sliding bits of pancake through the syrup pooled on her plate. Carole was greeted with half-hearted 'hellos.' Only Mike greeted her with a smile.

"Wanna pancake?"

"Maybe later," Carole told him, smiling back.

David and Tad couldn't offer her a greeting because they were racing to see who could down his glass of juice first. Carole assumed that Katy was sleeping in the bassinet against the far wall—though she didn't know how with the racket in the room.

"Start eating those pancakes," Brian barked, sitting down next to Tina's high chair. "Come on, baby," he urged. "Eat."

Tina shook her head. "I want her to feed me," she said, pointing to Carole.

"That's Ms. Chapman," Brian said.

"Can I give you a kiss?" Tina asked, ignoring her brother. "Daddy didn't give me a kiss."

Carole felt a tug on her heartstrings.

"Tina!" Lisa cried. "Daddy was in a hurry. He told us it was an emergency, and he blew us all a kiss. Now leave Ms. Chapman alone."

"She's fine," Carole said, approaching the highchair. "And why don't you all call me Carole. It'll be easier."

"That's great," Brian said. "Look, do you mind feeding her, Carole? I still have to shower. I'm running late because I had to fix breakfast."

How hard could it be to feed a three-year old? "Of course I don't mind."

"Thanks," he called, already heading for the door. "You're a lifesaver."

Carole took Brian's place and offered Tina a bite of pancake. The little girl smiled at her, a smile so like Chris's it stole Carole's breath...and just the slightest bit of her heart.

"I wanna kiss first," Tina insisted.

"Of course," Carole said, leaning over to kiss Tina's plump cheek. To her surprise, Tina's chubby hands reached out, one resting on the sleeve of Carole's silk shirt, the other pressing against her cheek.

"Holy cow, Tina! Look what you've done!' Jake said in horror and disgust.

Carole drew back and looked at the sticky imprint of Tina's hand, complete with bits of gooey pancake on her expensive shirt. She felt like crying. She'd paid a small fortune for that shirt. Well, at least she was beginning to understand Chris's dress mode. She should have known better than to get dressed up for babysitting. Jeans—old jeans—would have been more suitable.

"It's all right. Really. I should have dressed more appropriately."

"I'll keen it up," Tina said, grabbing for her napkin. As she reached, she bumped her juice glass and sent it toppling over.

Before Carole could do more than gasp in surprise, orange juice cascaded off the edge of the tray, right into her lap.

"Tina!" four shocked voices chanted in perfect synchronization.

Automatically, Jake grabbed a dish towel from the cabinet top and thrust it at Carole. She looked up from the stain on her imported wool slacks and met Jake's wide-eyed gaze. The expression in his eyes was abject fear, fear of retribution that far exceeded the crime.

"I'm so sorry," he said. "She didn't mean to do it. It was an accident."

"I'm sorry," Tina and Sebastian echoed.

As Carole looked at Jake, a remnant of her conversation with Chris flitted through her mind. *"Jake's father beat him on more than one occasion."* Her heart constricted with pain. Jake was afraid she might react the same way his father had.

"Are you mad at me?" Tina asked, her pretty little mouth trembling, her eyes wide and tear-glazed.

Carole promptly offered them both a reassuring smile and took the towel Jake offered.

"No," she said to Tina, as she began to wipe up the spill. "I'm not mad at you. Accidents happen."

The relief on Jake's face would have been comical if it hadn't been so tragic. The collective sigh that issued from the children was audible. Carole added her own sigh to theirs. Sweet heaven! What had she gotten herself into? What time did Chris normally end his day?

She looked down at her soggy slacks. And what on earth was she going to wear the rest of the day?

CHAPTER SIX

Chris pulled into the driveway with a feeling of trepidation. Carole's red SUV was still there. Why? It was almost six and already dark. He'd supposed that she'd head home as soon as the older kids got in from school. But she hadn't, and for some inexplicable reason he was glad.

He wasn't sure how he felt about that. He tried not to think about the fact that Carole Chapman was the first woman since Val died who had interested him, which was absolutely insane since she wasn't his type at all. Nevertheless, he'd thought about her a lot over the weekend. She was a beautiful woman, and he was a man who could recognize and appreciate beautiful women even if there wasn't much opportunity for enjoying them. That should have been the end of it.

But despite her unfriendliness and the very basic differences in their approach to life, he'd wanted to see her again. Carole Chapman was a career woman with little to no knowledge, much less interest, in relating to or take care of a houseful of kids, an important factor when it came to women he dated. She was totally wrong for him and just as importantly, she was wrong for his family. He needed to put all that romantic nonsense out of his mind.

He'd sensed hostility in her that first night at the hospital, but it hadn't taken him long to realize that the resentment stemmed from some inner pain buried deep beneath the chic, efficient façade she presented to the world. At the time, he'd wished he had time to spend with her and see if he could get her to open up and tell him why she was hurting, but he'd been so busy signing papers to get temporary custody of Katy to give it much more than cursory thought.

Then, he'd been busy getting the baby settled into his crazy life and doing the never-ending, thousand-and-one things that had to be done on his days off that the weekend had slipped by without his ever getting a minute to look her up. By Sunday afternoon, he'd decided that was probably for the best. Carole Chapman wasn't his type, and if her scathing comment about his clothes was any indication, he certain wasn't hers. Carole was a Neiman Marcus kind of woman, and he was a Duluth Trading kind of guy. She was filet mignon; he was frozen fish sticks. She was a savvy businesswoman. He was just a cop looking for a woman as crazy as he was, someone who had a heart with enough love not only for him but for a hundred kids as well, give or take a few. Shoot, for all he knew, with her looks she could even be a 'player' as Brian, Jake and Lisa called them.

Then she'd surprised him by driving out to check on Katy and for better or worse his interest in her had piqued again. When things calmed down after Sunday's frog fiasco and he'd realized that Carole was actually sitting in his living room, his initial reaction was that she had come to check up on him, which he supposed she had. But since he'd felt her concern for Katy was genuine, it was okay.

He still couldn't believe the way she'd opened up and confided a bit about her past, but he supposed that finding a houseful of kids more or less in the same situation she'd once been in must have brought the painful memories back. Besides, everyone knew that sometimes it was easier to talk to a stranger than to someone you knew. The things she'd revealed about her past had helped him understand her attitude.

Chris suspected there weren't too many people who knew what she'd gone through as a child. He also figured she'd pursued financial success so single-mindedly not only for security but also to establish a feeling of self-worth and an identity, since she knew so little about who she really was, and what she did know left her feeling unwanted, unloved.

He sensed that she ached to be needed and loved. Everyone did. That's why he'd suggested she take care of the girls for a day. He might find out that his idea had ended in a disaster, but his heart whispered that he'd done the right thing by gently prodding her into babysitting the girls. There was no one more dependent than a baby, no one who gave so much unconditional love than a small child. Still, his plan might have backfired. Well, he'd soon know.

Chris opened the front door, murmuring a brief, fervent prayer that his scheme had worked.

"Dad's home!" Tad yelled the instant the

door closed behind him.

Like metal filings drawn to a magnet, kids flocked to the living room. Chris was vaguely aware of Katy crying in the kitchen.

"Daddy, we need to go look for a dress!" Lisa wailed.

Chris put his arm around her shoulders and gave her a hug. "Maybe tomorrow, huh? I'm beat, honey."

"I got an A plus," Mike announced, waving a school paper over his head.

"That's great!" Chris said, mussing the boy's hair.

"We went to the wildlife museum today, Dad and you shoulda seen the snakes and geela monster and stuff!" Tad cried in a voice brimming over with excitement.

"Gila," David corrected. "The G sounds like an H."

"Shut up, you four-eyed geek!" Tad said, elbowing David's ribs.

"Boys, please," Chris said, holding up his hands in surrender.

"Gimme a break!" Sebastian bellowed, hanging upside down on his perch.

"Yeah," Chris echoed. "Gimme a break."

He couldn't hold back the smile that claimed his lips at the bird's fitting commentary. Obviously Sebastian had heard the nightly argument often enough to know what came next.

"Tad, apologize to David and then go to your room. Thirty minutes. You know better than to call anyone names."

"But Dad!" Tad argued, even as David looked

on with unconcealed glee.

Chris met his son's outraged look with one of resoluteness. "Apology, please."

"Sorry," Tad said, though his voice held little remorse.

"Lose the attitude or I'll make it an hour. Go. And do your homework."

Without another word, Tad stalked down the hall toward his room.

With that fire stomped out, Chris bent over and swung Tina, who'd been tugging on his slacks, into his arms. "How's my baby girl?" he asked rubbing her tip-tilted nose with his.

"Good," she said with a giggle, planting a kiss on his cheek.

"Katy's got colic again." The calm statement came from Brian, who had just stepped through the swinging door.

"Wonderful," Chris replied, lowering Tina to the floor. Just what he needed to make his horrendous day complete.

"Homework, now," he said to the kids who parted at his command like the Red Sea.

Once, just once, it would be nice to come home to quiet—the old slippers-and-pipe routine, even though he didn't smoke. A little Giovanni playing softly in the background while he cuddled in front of the fireplace with a beautiful woman. An image of snuggling with Carole on the sofa flickered through his mind. Irritation banished it.

Dream on, Nicholas. Your romantic fantasy doesn't quite jibe with the life you've chosen. And the woman is certainly wrong.

His mind set straight, at least for the moment, he squared his shoulders to face the chaos in the kitchen. The sight that greeted him stopped him mid-stride just inside the door.

With Katy cradled in her arms, Carole paced the heart pine floor. She'd discarded her shoes, and one bright red toenail poked through the sheer trouser socks she wore. Her silk blouse—which had cost a hundred bucks if it cost a penny—boasted a big stain of some sort on the sleeve. Instead of the slacks he expected to see, she wore a pair of Lisa's sweat pants that were a few inches too short for Carole's long legs. He was afraid to ask what had happened to the pricy slacks.

Her hair, usually sleek perfection, was pulled back in a ridiculously short ponytail that stuck out at the nape of her neck. Her customarily impeccable makeup was reduced to smears of mascara around her tired-looking brown eyes.

She glanced up and saw him in the doorway. They stared at each other across the room.

"Are you all right?" he asked, starting toward her.

She nodded, but her bottom lip trembled the same way Tina's did when she was trying not to cry. Chris fought the urge to gather both Carole and Katy into his arms.

"Something's wrong with Katy," she said in a quavering voice.

"Probably colic."

"That's what Brian said. She's been crying for an hour, and I didn't know what to do. I tried to give her a bottle, but she wouldn't take it. I can't stand for her to hurt, and I just didn't know what to do," she repeated, her voice catching on a sob. "I tried to tell you I couldn't do this."

He watched her face crumple and her model-straight shoulders slump. Tears filled her dark eyes and began to slide down her pale cheeks. Chris didn't think; he acted. Half a dozen steps took him to her and, without a word he did the very thing he'd wanted to do earlier. He took her in his arms and drew her close, Katy sandwiched between them.

His big hand cupped her ponytail, and he drew her head down till her forehead rested against his chest. The faint, mingled scents of maple syrup and baby spit up assailed him. In a gesture he recalled from his marriage, he pulled the rubber band from her hair and began to knead the tight muscles at the base of her skull. His mouth moved against her sweet smelling hair, murmuring words of reassurance and comfort.

"Shh. Take it easy, honey. It's all right."

"I'm sorry," she sobbed.

"It isn't your fault. Katy's been having a tummy ache every night about this time."

Carole lifted her tear-ravaged face. "She has? I thought I'd done something wrong. She made a mess in her diaper and I had to give her a bath after all, and I was afraid I'd done something to hurt her."

"You did fine," he said over Katy's wailing. "Babies are tougher that you think."

He released her and moved to the sink, where a roll of paper towels hung. He ripped one off, dampened it a little and tilted Carole's chin up. Gently, as if she were as young and delicate as Tina or Katy, he wiped away her tears. When he announced that he was finished and smiled at her, she smiled back, just a little.

"Come and sit down," he told her, ushering her to a chair near the end of the table. "I have some drops I can give her. I should have told you about them, but I was called away so early this morning that I forgot. Stay put. I won't be long."

In less than a minute, he was back, carrying a small bottle. He took Katy and deftly squirted the prescribed amount of medicine into her mouth. "There you go, pretty girl," he said, easing her up to his shoulder.

"What now?" Carole asked, wiping her palms on her slacks.

"We wait for the stuff to work," Chris told her as he sat down in a ladder-backed rocker near the wood-burning stove. He placed the baby across his knees and began to rub her back, patting and crooning soft words to her, the same way he had comforted Carole moments before.

She picked up the paper towel and blotted at her eyes again. "I must look a mess."

He shook his head. "Tired maybe. I'm sorry you had such a bad day."

She tucked a glossy strand of hair behind her ear and shrugged. "It wasn't so bad. Well, it wasn't *great*, but Tina was a big help."

"She's pretty good at fetching things," Chris agreed.

"She's an angel. I had no idea how smart three-year-old little girls could be."

"She is smart, thanks. And I know what you mean. It's like God put that woman thing in their DNA."

"I guess I missed out on that," Carole said with a wry smile. "He must have given me a bit of Marketing 101 instead."

Chris couldn't help laughing. The derisive comment was the first sign of humor he'd seen in her. "So how did you do with Katy—until this evening, I mean?"

"Okay I guess," she said hesitatingly. "I've been wondering..."

"What?"

Carole moved to stand beside the rocking chair. Reaching out, she placed her hand on Katy's downy blonde hair, stroking softly. "Do you think she misses her mother? Do you think she knows something's different?"

"I don't know. On some level maybe, though it can't be actual thoughts," he said. "Why do you ask?"

She shifted her gaze from Katy to Chris. "I don't want her to remember and hurt. I don't want her to grow up and feel the way I—" she paused "—that her mother...that no one loves her."

"She won't," Chris said, "because someone does love her."

"Really? Who?"

"You. Me. The kids."

She turned away, crossing her arms over her breasts. "I don't love her. I hardly know her."

"You don't have to *know* babies to love them. You just do."

"Maybe for some people. Not me."

"Then why are you so worried about her?" he asked. "Why were you so upset that something was wrong with her?"

Carole cast him a look over her shoulder. He could almost see her backbone stiffen. "I don't like to see anyone suffer. And while we're on the subject, you may as well know that I can't make a habit of missing work to take care of her. I have my own life."

"I understand."

"Good," she snapped. "Just so you do."

"Oh, I understand," he told her. "I understand perfectly. You're afraid to love her aren't you, Carole? Because if you do, her mother might come back and take her away, or she'll be sent somewhere and you'll never see her again. Isn't that right?"

Carole met his steady gaze. He was too smart, she thought. He saw right through her. And he was right. Very right. "Yes," she told him almost defiantly. "That's exactly what I'm afraid will happen."

"Come here. I want to show you something."

Reluctantly, Carole moved closer. Chris turned the now sleeping baby over.

"Look at her. Look at her and tell me that you refuse to love her."

Carole looked. Katy's face was flushed from crying, and her eyelashes lay like tiny fans against her cheeks. Her silky hair was damp, and one small fist was flung upward. Her fingernails were unbelievable small. She was perfectly beautiful and tiny and helpless. Carole felt the prickle of tears beneath her eyelids and let her gaze meet his.

Chris reached for one of her hands, which were clenched at her sides. "You have to let yourself feel, Carole. You have to open yourself up to the possibility of pain as well as pleasure."

"Why?" she cried, jerking her hand free of his disturbing touch. "Why should I take a chance of getting hurt?"

"Because every time you close up a part of yourself to the pain, you lose an equal capacity to feel love and pleasure. And you're far too beautiful and sensitive a woman not to live and love to the fullest."

Beautiful? He thought she was beautiful? It had been so long since she'd heard a compliment from a man that for an instant, she was in shock. And sensitive? She'd never thought of herself as sensitive. She did, however, have a sneaking suspicion there was something missing from her life, that she wasn't living it to the fullest.

She'd thought it was a man she needed, and maybe she'd been partly right. Maybe it was not only a man and physical fulfillment, but love and children. As exhausted as she was, and as trying and stressful as the day had been, the thought of leaving here and going to her lonely apartment was distasteful suddenly.

Get a grip on yourself, Carole. The man brainwashes for a living. Just because he's flattered you and because keeping a menagerie of kids is his thing doesn't mean that you should go all mushy inside and start thinking that a husband and family is what you need.

"I think you need to take an interest in something besides your shop," Chris said. "Do things you've never done before...see what the world has to offer. You have to make peace with your past if you ever hope to have a future. You might try giving love to someone, too, and just see if they don't give it back."

Peace with her past. That sounded like a mighty big order, but deep in her heart, she suspected he was right. Memory of what the dream Chris had shown her about her past and the people in her life flashed through Carole's mind, as it had intermittently throughout the day.

Guilt and confusion over doing the very thing she had accused other people of doing spread through her. Without meaning to, she had become Mabel Charmichael, except she didn't have any excuse for not visiting the children as Mabel had. Maybe she should go back and try to make amends for her inadvertent neglect.

They had been good to her at Fairhope. She'd been wrong to place any part of blame for her misery and shortcomings on the good people there. If she could just get past her fear of abandonment and find that peace she so needed, maybe she could give something more important than money. After all, it wasn't their fault no one had adopted her—or that she had been left there in the first place. As for loving someone...that sounded daunting too, especially with her disastrous history.

"Just pick someone to love, huh?" she said skeptically. "Like who?"

"My kids for starters," he said without a moment's hesitation. "Do you work next Saturday?"

A feeling of déjà vu swept over her. Was he going to ask her to baby-sit again? "No."

"Then why don't you come with us to hunt for a Christmas tree?"

A Christmas tree! She couldn't hide her surprise. She hadn't had a real tree since leaving the children's home, and she'd never gone to hunt for one. But with all the kids under his roof, of course Chris would have a tree, and probably a mountain of presents, too. She thought again of her cheerless apartment.

"Well," he said. "What do you say? Are you going to come along and do something to get out of your rut?"

Rut. He was right. She was in a rut. She went to work and she went home to solitary evenings spent doing...what? Maybe she would go on his family outing. She wasn't saying Chris was right about trying to love someone—that was going a bit too far—but she supposed it wouldn't hurt to tag along with the crazy clan to pick out a tree. It wasn't as if she had anything else planned.

CHAPTER SEVEN

Carole went down the wide steps of Fairhope toward the parking area. She was filled with a glow of contentment she'd never expected to feel. In fact, she wasn't sure she'd ever experienced this particular feeling. Surprising even herself, she'd taken the day off and driven the seventy miles to the children's home where she'd grown up. It seemed that ever since Chris Nicholas had come into her life, she'd embarked on more spur-or-the-moment actions than ever in her life.

At first, she'd convinced herself the trip had nothing to do with his suggestion that she make peace with her past and more to do with the ghost Chris's statement about her contributions to the orphanage. She'd never been able to tolerate hypocrisy, and she'd never connected that failing with herself. The dream had made her realize that she was no better than the people she'd always blamed for not caring enough. Right or wrong, she hadn't gone back to visit Fairhope because she'd built a new life and she hadn't wanted anything to remind her of the pain and disappointment of the old one.

But that was before she'd found Katy. Before she'd met Chris and the kids. Despite the fact that her determination and hard work had taken her far in life, finding Katy had enabled her past to catch up to her with a vengeance. Chris was right. She owed it to herself to try to come to terms with that past so that she could go on to a better future.

So she'd returned to Fairhope.

Her first stop was the administration building, where Tom Nelson still had an office. Though he had officially retired, he came in two days a week in an advisory capacity. He'd greeted Carole at the door with a brilliant smile of welcome and a hug. The familiar scent of the old-fashioned aftershave that always seemed to cling to him brought back a rush of good memories.

Since it was Wednesday, the older children were in school, but Mr. Nelson—who told her to call him Tom now that she was grown up—had taken Carole to see the preschoolers and infants. The sheer number of them saddened her, but at least she now realized that in many ways these children *were* fortunate. Children living destitute lives on the streets or with abusive, drug dependent parents were the ones to feel truly sorry for. As Chris pointed out, the children at Fairhope had a roof over their heads and three meals a day. Plus, the staff truly loved what they were doing. They loved kids. There was also the added plus that as a Christian home, they received a solid foundation during their years at Fairhope, both for the real world and the one to come. Carole had been so eager to get away that she hadn't realized that until now. Another of those pangs of remorse shot through her.

They went from building to building, Tom Nelson showing her the renovations, the additions and dredging up memories. As they talked and laughed, Carole realized with something of a start that she'd had a good life there. At the time, she had often been so wrapped up in herself that she hadn't fully appreciated the better moments or the many advantages.

As she was taken to the newly renovated kitchens and dining room, she recalled the times that she and some of the older girls had helped the cooks, preparing for the annual Christmas party. They had made dozens of cookies and decorated them with colored icing and sugar sprinkles, and shared lots of laughs while they were doing it.

There were the May Day baskets she'd made in elementary school and filled with flowers pilfered from the flower beds to leave on the doorsteps of the housemothers when they weren't looking, and decorating Valentine boxes and creating a special lacy card for the boy she happened to like.

There was the all-but-forgotten memory of her first formal dinner when she and Evelyn Hardy had stayed up until after midnight revamping a hand-me-down party dress. It had been fun, she realized now. And she recalled feeling and looking very pretty in it. Now, at the end of the day, she was a little surprised to realize that she sent money *not* just because she felt obligated for what the home had done for her, but because she *was* grateful and she did care. She'd always cared on some deeper level, but staying away was the only way she could protect her heart from the painful memories.

As she drove home, Carole's thoughts traveled back over other aspects of the day. Tom had insisted she stay to meet the school kids and she was somehow cajoled into staying for supper.

After the prayer, which brought tears to her eyes, Tom got up and introduced her, telling the residents that she was a former Fairhope girl and what a success she had made of herself. Both humbled and proud, and wanting to show camaraderie with the current residents, she volunteered to be a runner for the meal.

It had been fun sitting at the long table with the bowls of stew, platters of hot bread and pitchers of lemonade passing among eager hands. As the bowls and pitchers were emptied, it had been her job to "run" to the kitchen to get them refilled.

After one of her runs, she had propped her elbows on the table to talk to a boy across from her, and the dining room had suddenly rung with well over a hundred voices singing a refrain she thought she'd forgotten.

"Get your elbows off the table, Carole Chapman! Get your elbows off the table, Carole Chapman! We have told you once or twice that it isn't very nice. Get your elbows off the table, Carole Chapman!"

She'd blushed and laughed, feeling at one with the children of Fairhope.

Before leaving, she had wanted to ask Tom about the Bradleys, but at the last minute she changed her mind. What did it matter now? Her visit had been a memorable experience, and she promised herself she would repeat it soon.

Unaware that she was humming the "elbows" song, she pulled into her usual parking at the apartment complex, certain that she'd done the right thing.

Saturday, December 3

The day dawned cold and crisp and sunny. As Carole tramped around the tree farm, she was thankful she'd dressed in warm jeans and her red wool jacket. It was lovely December weather, and looking for the prefect Christmas tree with the Nicholas clan was quite an experience. She only regretted that Katy and Lisa, who had a bit of a sore throat, hadn't been able to come. They'd been left at home in the capable hands of Mrs. Landry.

Lisa had been fine on Thursday evening. Carole had been ringing up a big sale when she'd looked up to see the all Nicholas family troop into The Ultimate Man. She didn't miss the curious, considering glances from her staff or the looks of approval when their gazes lighted on Chris.

They had come to the mall to shop for Lisa's dress and to try to find something for Jake, who was going on his first "date" to a church Christmas party. Though they hadn't met with success for Lisa, Carole found something just right for Jake's "coming out." Then, in high spirits, they had all trekked to the food court, where Chris treated them to a fast food dinner and invited her to share their Christmas Day meal at noon.

She had to think about that for a moment. She was smart enough to realize that the gesture meant nothing more than Chris knowing she would spend the day alone and his caring heart didn't want her to be lonely. That's the kind of man he was. All she had to look forward to was dinner for one and a day alone in her apartment, which sounded like a dismal way to spend a holiday. But that was the way she'd spent all her Christmases since she'd been on her own, and it had never bothered her before. So, knowing that she was digging a deeper hole for her heart but unable to say no, she'd agreed.

The whole family seemed thrilled by her acceptance. Carole couldn't remember when she'd ever had such a delicious chicken sandwich or laughed so much or heard so much good-natured teasing and felt such closeness and love. However, she'd had mixed feelings upon learning that Chris's parents were arriving from Dallas three days before Christmas and that his mother would fix a traditional holiday dinner, complete with all the trimmings. She wasn't sure she was ready to meet his parents, especially when she was nothing to him but one of his rescues.

"Hey! Come look at this one!" Brian yelled from several yards away, shattering both Carole's pensive mood and her nagging thoughts. He and Jake had been foraging ahead among the rows of evergreens, carrying the saw and a measuring rod.

Chris waved at the boys and turned to

Carole. "I'm glad you're back."

Shielding her eyes from the bright sunlight, she looked up at him. Her heart skipped a beat at the warmth she saw in his eyes. She sighed. Chris Nicholas was an extremely handsome man, and she'd spent way too much time thinking about him this past week.

Even though she couldn't recall having felt precisely this way before, she likened her seesawing emotions to what a teenager with a crush must suffer. She refused to consider that her feelings might represent more than that, even though something deep inside whispered that she was fooling herself. She'd dreaded spending the day with him, yet contrarily, she could hardly wait for Saturday to come. And now that it had, she was even more confused by her feelings.

"What do you mean, back?"

"You were here in body, but your thoughts must have been on another planet. Want to talk about it?" he asked.

She shook her head. He was way too good at figuring her out as it was. If he knew she was the slightest bit interested in him, he'd probably die of mortification.

"It was nothing," she assured him. "I was just thinking about...things."

Chris reached out and brushed a stray lock of hair away from her mouth. His touch was gentle and lingering and kindled more of those feelings Carole knew she'd be better off not feeling. She resisted the urge to hold his hand against her face and beg him to explain what was happening to her.

"Hmm," he said, "sounds serious. And we aren't here to be serious. We're here to show you that hunting for a Christmas tree is fun and that parenting eight kids can be an almost normal state. No more serious thoughts, okay?"

"Okay," she agreed with a hesitant smile.

For a moment it seemed as if he couldn't look away. His blue gaze caressed her face, lingering on her lips. She knew it was a silly thought, but she imagined that she could almost feel the touch of his mouth against hers. Her tongue skimmed over her lips, moist with gloss.

The involuntary action seemed to break the spell binding them. His eyes aglow with tenderness, Chris shifted Tina, who was sitting on his shoulders. "Come on sweetheart, let's go find a tree."

Puzzled, Carole watched as he turned and started toward Brian and Jake. She knew he'd been speaking to Tina, but he'd been looking straight into *her* eyes.

"It's the prettiest tree we've ever had!" Lisa said two hours later, as she placed another ornament just so.

"It is, isn't it?" Chris agreed. He shot Carole a crooked smile. "We say that every year, but every year, I think it's the truth."

Carole, who held Tina on her lap, smiled back before returning her gaze to their handiwork. Brian and Jake had indeed found the perfect tree and had taken turns sawing it off at the base. Chris had helped load it into the pickup that Brian had driven to the tree farm. Carole, along with the rest of the Nicholas gang, had packed into Chris's nearly new SUV and they'd headed back to the farm to start decorating.

Lisa helped Carole fix sandwiches while the guys fitted the tree in the stand and strung the lights. After they'd finished eating, all hands set to adding the ornaments—from handmade construction-paper chains to an exquisite crystal sphere. Sebastian paraded back and forth, generally making a nuisance of himself and crowing, "A par-tri-hige in a pear treeeee!"

"I want to help," Tina cried, obviously feeling as if she was missing out on the fun.

"You're too little," Tad told her.

Tina turned to her father and planted her little hands on her hips. "Uh-*uh*! I am not, am I, Daddy?"

"Of course you aren't," Chris said, producing a small wooden bear from the ornament box. "You can hang this one."

He picked her up, handed her the bear and showed her where to place the wire hanger. "This is the one Mommy bought for you just before you were born," he told her.

"You said I don't have a Mommy," Tina reminded him. "Why not?"

Every eye in the room focused on Chris.

"Don't you remember what I told you?" he asked.

"You said she went to live in heaven. Why? Didn't she like living here with us?"

"Of course she did. She loved being here with you and Lisa and Tad," he said, his voice huskier than it had been mere seconds before.

"And you?"

"And me. But Jesus needed her, so she went to live in heaven and left you for me to love instead."

Taking the explanation at face value, Tina nodded and hung the bear. Then she looked at her father, her blue eyes wide and innocent. "I want a mommy," she said. "Please, Daddy."

"Finding a mommy isn't as easy as going to the grocery store and picking out your favorite kind of cookies," Lisa told her baby sister.

"Please, Daddy," Tina cajoled, undaunted. "Carole could be my mommy."

Chris made brief eye contact with Carole who felt her face grow hot with embarrassment and her throat tighten with unshed tears. Tina's suggestion was one of the nicest compliments she'd ever received.

"Well, that's a pretty good suggestion," he said, "but Carole may have other ideas about a family. We'll find a mommy for you someday, sweet pea," he said, rubbing Tina's nose with his. "I promise."

"I promise," Sebastian squawked, his timely interruption drawing attention away from Tina's wistful plea.

"Look," Tad said, pointing to the Christmas tree. "Sebastian is our tree-top decoration!"

All eyes turned to the parrot perched at the very tip top of the tree. He bobbed his head up and down, almost as if he were taking a bow.

Thankfully, the action elicited a round of laughter from the onlookers and eased the tension in the room. Even Tina giggled, her request momentarily forgotten.

"Just who to you think you are, you crazy bird?" Brian asked, his hands planted on his hips.

"A par-tri-hige in a pear treeeee! The bird croaked.

As coincidental as it was, Sebastian's pronouncement sent everyone into another round of laughter.

When the furor subsided, Tina demanded that Chris give her back to Carole. As she took his daughter from Chris's arms, Carole's gaze met his. She tried to look away, but couldn't,

"She's really getting attached to you," he told her. And in a whisper, he added, "And all the boys have a crush on you."

"All of them?" *Even you?*

"All of them."

"But I thought Brian had a girlfriend," she said, matching his low tone.

"He does, and so does Jake, but that doesn't mean they can't find you attractive too. I guess they like the all the advice you give them on their clothes and stuff." He grinned.

"Oh," Carole said with a slight smile back. "I'm afraid I'm not too familiar with the way males think."

"Stick around. You'll figure it out in no time."

Stick around. Heaven knew she wanted to, but she wasn't certain where all this was leading. She hadn't even had the courage to tell Chris about her trip to Fairhope yet. She had a feeling he would approve and that he would know exactly how she'd felt when she left. He would recognize the peace the trip had brought her. He would be thrilled about the changes taking place inside her.

But she herself wasn't so sure about those changes. Chris Nicholas had come into her life and turned it topsy-turvy. He'd made her think about and face things she hadn't thought she could deal with. But what would happen when he was finished "rescuing" her? What would happen when there were no more ghosts in her past? Would he still be eager for her company, her friendship?

The fear that he wouldn't filled her with a sudden inexplicable sorrow, even though she wasn't certain she wanted Chris for a friend. She was afraid that her feelings, despite her firmest intentions, were swiftly mutating from wary friendliness to something more—something she was afraid to take too close a look at.

CHAPTER EIGHT

Tuesday, December 6

The Ultimate Man. Carole speaking. May I help you?"

"Hi."

The softly spoken greeting sent shivers of pleasure scampering throughout her. "Hi," she replied a trifle breathlessly. "How are you?"

"Other than facing a stack of paperwork a mile high, I'm fine," Chris said. "What about you. Any aftereffects from the day spent at the Nicholas zoo?"

Laughing with happiness, Carole denied any ill effects.

"Are you working tonight?" he asked.

"That depends."

"On what?"

"Whether or not you want me to baby-sit," she teased.

He laughed. "No, I don't want you to baby-sit. I want you to come to dinner."

"Dinner?" she echoed, unable to hide her surprise.

"Yeah."

"Then, no. I'm not working, and I'd like very much to come."

"Good," he said. "Is six-thirty okay?"

"Fine."

"I'll see you then."

Carole ended the connection but the silly smile she was wearing refused to disappear.

"It was wonderful lasagna," Carole said as she and Chris carried their coffee cups into the living room. They'd left clean-up duty to the kids.

"Thank you. Maybe you'll return the honor sometime."

Carole felt overwhelmed. "I'm not certain I'd know how to feed this many people."

Chris smiled at her over the rim of his cup. "Then we'll have to make it just the two of us."

More confused than ever, she set her cup on the coffee table and sank into the wing chair across from the sofa. "That would be...nice."

"In the meantime, would you like to go with us to see the Christmas play at the kids' school? Tad, Mike and David all have parts."

"When is it?" she asked. "If I'm not working, I'd love to go."

"Friday night at seven-thirty."

"I don't have to work, so I—"

"Daddy," Lisa interrupted from the doorway. "Can I talk to Carole a minute?

"Sure," Chris said. "Come on in."

Lisa sat beside her father and leaned toward Carole. "I need to ask you about Kyle's tuxedo. Should he wait until I get my dress—" this was accompanied by a pointed look at her father "—before he chooses a style and color?"

Carole nodded. "It would be best, unless he goes with black. He can't go wrong with that, no matter what you wear."

Lisa stood, a look of relief on her pretty face. "Thanks. I knew you'd know. I'll tell Kyle."

"Just a minute, young lady," Chris said. "In all fairness, I think you should tell Carole that I've taken you several places to look for a dress, but we haven't found anything yet."

"That's true," Lisa said, leaning over and kissing his cheek. "You're an okay guy, Mr. Nicholas."

"Thanks," he said dryly. "Now get back in there and finish the dishes while I entertain my guest."

Lisa shot him a playful look and glanced at Carole. "By all means," she said, heading toward the kitchen.

Friday, December 9

The school gymnasium was packed. Chairs had been set up facing the stage at one end, and the families of the performers noisily filled every row. According to the program, the play was called *A Visit to the North Pole*. Some of the children were featured in a speech choir, reciting quatrains about various toys, which then came to life courtesy of other costumed kids.

David, middle ways of the back row of the speech choir, caught sight of Chris and Carole and waved. They waved back, and then cheered as Tad, along with several other youngsters marched onstage in full military regalia while the music teacher played the "March of the Toy Soldier."

Mike was a superb robot, complete with flashing lights.

When the play was over and refreshments were being served in the library, the boys rushed up to Carole and Chris, wide smiles on their faces. They couldn't wait to introduce Carole to their teachers, who looked at Chris and Carole the same way Lisa had. The same way her staff at the store had. Though Carole was embarrassed, a quick glance at Chris told her was taking their speculation in stride.

The memory of his expression stayed with Carole as they took the boys to McDonald's for milk shakes. Did everyone assume that she and Chris were an item? Were her growing feelings for him that obvious? She shuddered at the thought that she was so transparent and vowed to clamp down on her growing feelings for him. After all, there was no sense falling for a man who was so happy with his situation.

Saturday, December 10

Carole rose before daybreak and stirred up a double batch of sugar cookie dough, since the kids wanted to give cookies to all their friends. She was pretty excited about making cookies with them, especially with the memories of the good times at Fairhope fresh in her mind. Armed with cookie cutters, food coloring, two bags of powdered sugar and a variety of sprinkles, she headed for the Nicholas farm.

Chris, his fair hair uncombed and sporting a twenty-four hour growth of beard, met her at the door. He looked rumpled and sleepy and so wonderfully male that Carole's heart missed a beat. He held a cup of coffee in one hand.

"Hi," he said, stepping aside for her to enter. "I saw you coming up the drive and thought you could use this." He held out the mug of fragrant brew.

"Thanks." She relinquished her bag of baking supplies to him and took the proffered coffee.

"Are you sure about doing this?" he asked, his eyes twinkling as if he knew something she didn't

"Sure," she said blithely. "Why wouldn't I be?"

He only smiled that sweet smile and made a sweeping gesture toward the kitchen island. "It's all yours."

Three hours later, Carole knew the answer to that question, as well as why Chris had volunteered to watch Katy. Somehow Carole had survived what seemed like an endless battle over who got which cookie cutter, who was using which color icing, and who had what sprinkles. Not to mention trying to keep a parrot off the table. Thank goodness Chris stuck his head in the door every now and then to subdue the more vehement arguments.

She watched numbly as Tad licked some red icing off the spreader he was using to frost a cookie. She sighed. Oh, we'll, what were a few germs among family members? Mike was calmly licking up the chocolate sprinkles he'd shaken into his palm, all thoughts of decorating gone from his mind. Who cared? They were finishing up the last batch. All that was left was the cleaning up.

Carole's gaze drifted around the kitchen. She stifled a groan of dismay. Blobs of icing dotted the table and floor, faces and clothes. Sebastian had made a flyover above the island where she'd been cutting out the cookies and a fine powdering of flour floated in the air, leaving a film over everything within a five-foot radius. She was exhausted and she still faced a mammoth cleanup operation. Still despite everything, the smiles she'd seen throughout the day made it all worthwhile.

"Don't eat those!" Brian said to Tina, who was plucking dragées from the front of a white-frosted snowman.

"I like them," Tina argued, popping one of the tiny silver balls into her mouth.

"I don't care if you do. You're not supposed to eat them! They have metal on them, for crying out loud! Dad!" he yelled, heading for the door.

"Spit it out, please," Carole said with an encouraging smile. "It could make you sick."

"Okay." Tina obediently spit the confection onto the table.

Carole automatically reached for a paper towel.

"Tina!" Chris bellowed from the doorway, a thunderous look on his face.

"Yes, Daddy," Tina said, the picture of innocence as she looked up at him.

"She spit it out," Carole told him, averting a possible tearful confrontation between Chris and his daughter. She'd learned that Tina was incredibly sensitive to reprimands.

"Oh. Good." He looked around the room in disbelief. "Good grief! It looks like the Pillsbury Doughboy and a few of his friends had a really wild party in here."

"I'm sorry," Carole said, pushing her hair away from her face.

"It's not your fault." Planting his hands on his hips, he faced the true offenders. "Go get cleaned up, gang. I'll help Carole with this."

"We're not finished!" Tad cried.

"Oh, yes you are. Now git!"

The room emptied of kids, and Carole sank into a vacated chair, so tired she was oblivious to the blob of frosting in the seat.

"I tried to tell you this was going to be madness," Chris said, moistening a paper towel.

Carole looked up at him. "As I recall, you asked me if I was sure I wanted to do it."

"Same thing," he said, squatting beside her.

"What's wrong?" she asked, fighting the temptation to lean away from his nearness, simply because it made her feel all quivery inside.

"You look like one of the kids you have so much flour on your face."

She offered him a wry smile. "I imagine I do."

Grasping her chin in gentle fingers, Chris

began to wipe away the flour. She lowered her lashes in an attempt to hide the pleasure his touch evoked.

"You have the most beautiful complexion," he commented in a soft voice, dabbing at a white smudge near her mouth. "And the most incredible mouth I think I've ever seen."

The words sent her gaze flying to his. He was so close that she could see the darker flecks of blue in his eyes. Too close! Carole swallowed hard as his face moved even closer. He was going to kiss her! she thought on a wave of excitement and panic.

"Hey, Dad!" Tad called, pushing through the swinging door.

"What?" Chris snapped, somehow managing to put several inches between him and Carole.

Tad came to a halt just inside the door. "Are you kissin' her?"

"No," Chris said, standing, "I am not kissing her. I was washing the flour off her face."

Tad grinned. "Yeah, she's a sight, all right."

"What do you want, Tad?" Chris asked with extreme patience.

"I wanna know if I can have a boa constrictor for Christmas. Lisa said you wouldn't let me."

"Lisa is right."

The sound of Tina crying in the living room filtered through the door.

"What now?" Chris grumbled to no one in particular. He tossed the paper towel onto the cluttered table on his way to the living room.

Carole sighed and stood up, uncertain of all but one thing. It looked as if she would be cleaning up by herself after all.

Thursday, December 15

On Thursday night, Katy stayed with a baby-sitter while the Nicholas crowd went Christmas caroling with a group from their church. Carole joined them, but her mind wasn't on singing. It was on the kiss Chris had almost given her on Saturday, and the fun she'd had as he and Lisa helped her clean up the cookie mess.

It hadn't escaped her attention that she was spending a lot of time with Chris and his family—and loving every minute of it, even though she felt out of her depth most of the time. Monday night they had again gone looking for Lisa's dress, but Brian had a rescheduled basketball game, and their time together was cut short. Carole thought she saw regret in Chris's eyes when he'd told her goodbye. But whatever *he* was feeling she knew that *she* was falling hard for *him*. It was stupid. Ridiculous. But she didn't seem to be able to help herself. This was the point when she would usually walk away from the relationship, but she couldn't bring herself to do that just yet.

"Having fun?" Chris asked.

"As a matter of fact, I am. It reminds me of when I was a kid and the children's home use to..." she paused, realizing that she'd found another happy moment in her past.

"What?" he asked.

"I went to Fairhope Chris," she told him in a rush.

He nodded but didn't seem surprised. "How did it go?"

"Good. It was good." She still couldn't believe it had turned out so well. "I realized a lot of things while I was there, among them the fact that it wasn't such a bad place. I remembered a lot of good times, and I think the people there really cared. Care."

Chris looked thoughtful for a moment. "I'm glad you went. I think it was a good move. A responsible, mature move. And I think it's going to open up a whole new world for you."

Carole hoped so. She offered him a tremulous smile.

"And, under the circumstances, I think it's okay for me to ask you a question."

"Sure. Anything," she said, wondering what it could be.

"I've been invited to a party Saturday night. It's going to be a black-tie affair with a lot of political bigwigs in attendance."

"Do you need me to help you pick out your tux?" she said, seizing on the first thing that came to mind.

"No. I want you to go with me."

Carole looked at him, dumbfounded. "You want me to go with you?"

He shrugged and nodded.

Carole thought he looked a little unsure of himself, a first for Chris Nicholas, she knew.

"I'm asking you for a date. I figure you've seen the kids, seen things at their worst. You haven't taken off running and screaming yet, so chances are you won't." He blew out a deep breath. "So, what do you say, Carole Chapman? Will you be my date?"

She nodded, a quiet joy filling her. "I say yes."

CHAPTER NINE

Carole's gown was strapless black velvet with a center slit in the back that revealed her shapely calves when she walked. A moiré sash swathed her slim hips and was gathered into a huge bow on the left. Her hair was pulled sleekly back to the nape of her neck, where black silk flowers nestled becomingly. The style showed off her diamond drop earrings, the only jewelry she wore. Her nails were painted Drop Dead Red, and her perfume was the dramatic scent of Opium.

She was ready a full thirty minutes early.

And she was a nervous wreck.

The gala, hosted by a prominent state politician, would be a showcase for the area's social élite. It was even rumored that the governor would make an appearance. Chris had been invited because of the invaluable work he had done for the police force. Although psychologists had long been part of many law-enforcement teams, their unique contributions were only recently being recognized and applauded by the public.

Carole checked her makeup for the tenth time and wondered what she could possibly say to people of the social strata she would be encountering during the evening. If it wasn't so near time for Chris she would call him and cancel. As she glanced at the clock to see if that was a possibility, the doorbell rang. Casting a final look in the mirror, she went to greet her date.

Date. The thought that she had a date with Chris was almost impossible to believe.

He stood before her in a black tuxedo that fit him to perfection. Why, she wondered a bit dazedly, had she ever thought the man had no clothes sense? She couldn't have done better if she'd chosen his attire herself. She registered a brief impression of a pleated white shirt and got a whiff of some exotic men's cologne before she heard him say, "You're beautiful."

Her gaze climbed from his wide chest over the black tie to the cleft in his chin, past his mouth and his freshly shaved cheeks to his tender blue eyes.

"You don't look so bad yourself," she said in a breathless whisper.

His lazy smile sent the corners of his mouth crawling upward. "Not 'reprehensible'?"

Carole felt a blush creep over her face at his reference to her rudeness the night they'd first met. "Are you ever going to let me live that down?"

"Probably not," he told her, his eyes sparkling with a teasing light. "I have to have some defense, puny as it may be. Are you ready?"

Carole nodded, wondering what he meant about defenses. Obviously, though he didn't intend to discuss it now.

"Just let me get my wrap," she said. "I won't

be but a minute."

Carole leaned back against the leather upholstery of Chris's SUV and drew in a contented, weary sigh. The venue for the event had been crowded, and much to her surprise, she hadn't felt uncomfortable at all. Actually, she'd known a great many of the people in attendance as regular customers at The Ultimate Man. In spite of her fears that she wouldn't fit in, several guests praised her business savvy and thanked her for carrying a line of quality clothing that made shopping trips to Dallas unnecessary.

Chris had been an attentive date, fetching her food and helping her eat it, teasing and just being his charming self. There had been a string quartet and dancing, but Carole had declined, since she'd never been comfortable on a dance floor. Chris didn't seem to mind and said he was like a hippo in a mud bog when he tried to dance. As he'd known it would, the analogy had made her laugh, so they'd attempted a couple of slow dances.

Now they rode to the apartment in silence, almost as if both were afraid words would break the spell binding them. Carole knew the hour was approaching midnight and wondered if, at the chiming of the hour, she, like Cinderella, would be left with nothing but her memories. Then, out of nowhere, Chris's earlier comment slipped into her thoughts. *I have to have some defense...*

Was it ridiculous to think that he was as attracted to her as she was him?

At her apartment door, she was filled with doubts and questions. Should she ask him in? Or was he ready to go home? She could make some coffee, or...

"Defense against what?" she heard herself say as she swung the door open.

"You," he said easily, letting her know the subject was on his mind, too.

She looked at him in wonder, afraid to hope he meant what he seemed to mean. Before she could gather her wits and formulate her next question, he grasped her bare shoulders and propelled her into the apartment and toward the large mirror hanging over the gray sofa.

"Look at you," he said to their reflections. "How could any man not go a little crazy over a woman like you?"

But Carole wasn't looking at herself. She was looking in the silvery glass at *him* as he stood behind her, his big hands cupping her shoulders. Their gazes meshed in the mirror.

"And are you?" she asked in a quavering voice, "a little crazy over me?"

"Yeah," he said with another of those disarming smiles, his hands skimming from her shoulders to her elbows and back. "I am. Maybe more than a little. How do you feel about that?"

"I...I don't know," she said honestly.

He turned her toward him, took her face in his hands and slowly lowered his mouth to hers. His lips were firm, yet incredibly soft. Sparks like tiny electrical shocks flickered throughout her and she gave a shuddering sigh that was lost as Chris deepened the kiss. Her arms slid around his waist, and she leaned into his wide chest. It had been forever since she'd been kissed, and never like this. Never by a man she loved so much...

The thought entered her mind willy-nilly, unexpected, certainly unwanted. Love? Surely not. The realization that she'd done the unthinkable and fallen in love with him had the effect of cold water thrown in her face. When and how had she let it happen? Oh, she'd known she was playing with fire by spending so much time with him and his family, but she'd really thought she could walk away when the time came, since she knew better than to let herself care too much.

Her lifelong fear rose up inside her. Fear that she would give her all to him and when he realized she wasn't the wife he needed for his crazy family, and that she was lacking in something vital in her makeup would cause him to walk away just as everyone else had. She drew away from him, knowing that she had to disconnect from his touch or be lost forever, though she suspected that it was too late.

"What is it?" he asked, sensing not only her physical pulling away but her emotional withdrawal.

When she refused to look at him, he grasped her chin in his hand, forcing her gaze upward. Her eyes were dark with anguish and swimming with tears.

"I'm sorry," she whispered. "I can't do this."

"What? Share a kiss?"

She made a vague gesture. "Us. This. Whatever it is."

He didn't speak for long seconds. The only sound she heard was the painful beating of her breaking heart.

"I understand," he said at last. "I've rushed you. I mean, we really haven't known each other very long, but I—" He paused, and his lips twisted in a wry smile. "I have no excuse except that you're the first woman to interest me since Val... I'm sorry."

Carole closed her eyes and clamped her lips together to keep from crying. She felt his mouth touch hers with feather softness, felt the warm vapor of his breath against her cheek as he said, "I'll give you time. I'll give you all the time you need."

She placed her palm against his cheek and opened her eyes to look into his. Her heart was breaking. She'd taken his advice. She'd offered her love and her heart to someone. Him. To all of them. Carole knew that if she stayed around him long enough she would be unable to resist the pull of him and his wonderful family, unable to resist loving all of them.

She was a coward, too afraid of being hurt to take a chance on what he was offering, which left only one thing to do. Walk away right now, the way she always did, before she could figure out how wrong she was for him and the kids and leave her for someone more suitable.

"Time won't help, Chris," she said, softly, tilting up her chin in a show of pride.

Chris reacted like a man, not a psychologist.

Taking her shoulders again, he gave her a gentle shake. "Don't do this, Carole," he pleaded. "Please don't do this. I know you care for me, whether you admit it or not. I feel it when I kiss you and I see it in your eyes."

"Maybe so," she acknowledged. "But it will go away." *When I'm dead and buried.*

He looked as if she'd slapped him. "Why would you say something like that?"

"Because it's true. Some people might find a lasting love, but statistics show that the opposite is true for most people. And when the feelings go, so does the other person. Besides, if you think about it, you know that I'm not cut out for country living or a passel of kids."

He gave a slow nod. "I see. You've got things all figured out. But you're wrong, Carole, so wrong." He stepped away from her. "I suppose I should be mad, but instead I feel sorry for you. You could have a life with people who love you if you'd only let go of your fear. I'm not your mother, and I'm not any other man you've cared for. I believe in commitment. Despite what you think, you're a very lovable person. If you weren't, I'd never have fallen in love with you."

Without another word, he turned, crossed the room and let himself out.

His parting words didn't sink in until she heard the sound of his car engine starting. Carole lifted a trembling hand to stifle the harsh sob fighting its way up her throat. She glimpsed her reflection in the mirror. What she saw was a woman, her broken heart reflected in the dark eyes brimming with tears.

It was better this way, she thought as the moisture spilled down her cheeks. Chris said he loved her, but it was probably nothing more than the circumstances that had brought them together. Why should he love her? What did she possibly have to offer him and his kids? No, it was better that she hurt a little now than for her to give herself to him and hurt a lot later.

CHAPTER TEN

Wednesday, December 22

The four days since Chris had walked out her door were the longest Carole had ever lived through. She was short with customers, short with her help and miserable in general. She missed the kids—Brian's steadfastness, Lisa's chatter, Tad's and David's wrangling, Mike's sweetness, Tina's hugs and Jakes seriousness. She even missed Katy's crying.

But most of all, she missed Chris. Initially she wondered if he would call. After all, he'd said he loved her. But he hadn't called, and there was no way she could call him—not after the things she'd said.

Christmas was fast approaching. She'd thought this year would be different since he had invited her to spend the day with his family, and nervous yet excited, she'd bought everyone a gift. A few days ago, she'd sent the packages to the farm via UPS, but she hadn't heard a word from the Nicholas clan. It looked as if it would be the same old lonely Christmas for her after all. At home. Alone.

She picked up a glossy fashion magazine, hoping she might find something interesting enough to keep her from feeling sorry for herself at least for a while. Today was the day Chris's parents were due to arrive from Dallas. Carole envisioned them laughing, joking, hugging. Disgusted with her cowardice, she tossed the magazine onto the table and stretched out on the sofa. Maybe she could catch up on some rest. Sleep the afternoon away.

She drew the afghan up and closed her eyes, hoping that if she did sleep Chris wouldn't return as the ghost of Christmas future and show her just how empty the years ahead would be. She already suspected there would be precious little laughter or fun.

Chances were, there wouldn't be any love, either.

The phone was ringing. Carole struggled through a fog of sleep and reached for the receiver. Probably the store needing help with some problem or other. "Hello."

"Is this Carole Chapman?" a vaguely familiar voice asked.

"Yes," she said, pushing herself to one elbow. "Who's calling?"

"This is Officer Al Gibson."

She frowned. Al Gibson! What could the policeman who'd questioned her about finding Katy possibly want?

"Yes?" she queried in a wary voice. "What can I do for you?"

"Chris Nicholas called me a little while ago and asked if I'd give you a call. He needs you to come out to the farm right away."

"Why?" she asked, panic rising. "What's the matter?"

"I don't know," the officer said. "Something about one of the kids."

Carole's heart clenched. What could it be? Was Lisa sick again? Was someone hurt? And why hadn't Chris called himself? "Of course I'll go. I'm on my way. Thanks for calling."

It was a thirty-minute drive to Chris's farm, but breaking every speed limit put Carole in his driveway in twenty. She slammed the car door and raced up the steps. It was just dusk, and the geese must have already turned in for the night. She raised her hand to knock, but before her knuckles made contact with the wood, the door opened and Chris stood before her, tall and handsome and rugged-looking in his bright-red flannel shirt.

"What is it?" she asked in a rush. "What's wrong? Officer Gibson called and said you needed me. Something about one of the kids."

Chris nodded and Carole's heart took a nosedive.

He took her elbow and ushered her inside, closing the door behind them. Part of her noted conversation and Christmas music in the background and the wonderful scent of cinnamon in the air.

"Who is it?" she asked, swallowing hard. "Katy?"

"Yes," Chris told her with a nod. "It's Katy."

"What's wrong?"

"And Tina," he added.

"Tina?"

"And Tad and David and Mike."

For a moment, Carole was too stunned to speak. What could it be? A virus of some sort? Then she realized that Chris was perfectly calm. Too calm. It didn't make sense. If something was wrong with all the kids, wouldn't he be upset?

"Chris," she said softly. "What's going on? Al said—"

"I know what Al said. I asked him to call and told him what to say."

"What?"

"Hi Ca-role," Mike said, entering the room with his arms outstretched and a wide smile on her face.

"Hi, Mikey," Carole said, giving him an abstracted hug. She looked at Chris. "He seems fine to me. What's wrong?"

Before Chris could answer, Tad burst into the room.

"Hey, Dad, if I promise..." His voice trailed away when he saw Carole. Turning, he cupped his hands around his mouth and bellowed, "Hey everybody, Carole's here!"

The sound of chatting ceased and Carole heard the rest of the kids scrambling to get to the living room. One by one they entered, followed by a friendly looking older couple.

"Dad. Mom," Chris said. "This is Carole Chapman."

"Hello, Carole Chapman," an older version of Chris said, unknowingly repeating the very thing Chris had said to her at their first meeting.

"Hello, dear," Chris's mother said. "It's a

pleasure to meet you at last."

At last?

"Hi," Carole said, in a bit of a quandary. She turned toward Chris. "Chris—"

"I know. Something is supposed to be wrong, and it is. With all of us."

Her gaze scanned the sea of faces. Everyone looked fine to her.

"I need you, Carole," he said softly. "We all do."

"I'm having trouble with Kim," Brian said. "I swear I don't understand women."

Carole shot Chris a look. "I—I don't understand men, either."

"I need you to help me pick out a present for my mom if you have time," Jake said. "I don't know what to get her."

"I'd be glad to help you, Jake," Carole said, blinking fast to hold back the tears. She was beginning to understand what was going on, and her heart swelled with so much love she wasn't sure she could bear it. Chris was trying to show her that they wanted her to be a part of their lives, that they did need her.

"Will you *please* take me shopping?" Lisa wailed. "Daddy finally brought home this awful dress, and I just can't wear it! Kyle would refuse to be seen with me!"

Carole rolled her eyes. "After seeing a portion of your dad's wardrobe, I can only imagine!" she managed to joke. "Of course we'll go shopping. There will be some great after-Christmas sales."

"My sister sent me a new computer

program," David said, pushing his glasses up on his short nose, "and I can't figure it out. Do you think you could help me?"

Carole smiled at him. "I can try."

"Well I need someone to help me talk Dad into getting me a boa constrictor," Tad said.

"No!" Carole, along with everyone else, shouted.

"I need a hug," Mike said, putting his arms around Carole's waist.

"I need one, too," Tina said, making her way through her brothers to Carole who reached down and picked her up. "And I need a mommy. Reeeel bad," she tacked on.

Swallowing hard, Carole chanced another look at Chris before she squeezed Tina and set her on the floor. His blue eyes glowed with love.

"What about Katy?" she asked.

He grinned and Carole's heart turned over.

"I imagine she needs changing."

"And Chris needs a woman who can put up with all this," Chris's mother said. "So far, you seem to be a good candidate."

Carole looked at Chris's mother in surprise. Like everyone else in the room, the woman was smiling.

"How about it Carole?" Chris asked, taking her by the shoulders and drawing her close.

"How about what?" She wanted to make absolutely certain she wasn't misunderstanding.

"We want you to be a part of this family," he told her. "And I'm not talking about adoption."

Tears welled in her eyes, and she bit her lip to keep from crying.

"We love you Carole. Will you marry us?"

She looked around the room once more. Brian—girl problems. Lisa—boy problems. Tad. Pure mischief. And Mike with the sweet smile. It would be a challenge.

It would be hard.

It would be wonderful.

"Yes!" she cried, laughing and opening her arms to them all. "I'll marry you."

The kids rushed to her, laughing and shouting, each demanding her attention. Finally, an earsplitting whistle rent the air, and quiet reigned.

"What about *me?*" Chris asked.

Carole went willingly into his arms, and his mouth descended on hers in a promise as sweet as the future she now knew she would be hers.

"Wow."

"Look at that!"

"Hmmph!"

"Daddy!"

"Yuck!"

"Way to go, Chris!"

"Children...children! Maybe we'd all better go into the kitchen and leave them alone for a few minutes. "Come on, Tad."

"Aw, MeMe..."

"Now, Thaddeus."

"Yes'm."

The door closed behind the group, leaving Chris and Carole alone in the living room. He gave her a long, lingering kiss. When he pulled away, they were both breathless.

"Before the new year?" he asked, his eyes

glowing with love.

"Isn't that soon? We haven't known each other that long, and I really don't know how to be a wife, much less a mother."

"No woman knows how to be a mother until she becomes one. I know what I need to know, and that's that you love my family, and me, and we all love you. If things get tough, God will help us get through them."

Carole looked up into his eyes for long seconds. There was no doubt there. Not even a smidgen. "Yes," she said at last. "Before the new year."

Chris kissed her again, a kiss that sealed their commitment, proved their love.

"Way to go, Chris!" the parrot croaked from his perch atop the lemon tree.

Chris drew back and glanced toward the tree. "Thanks, Sebastian. Glad you approve."

And Carole laughed

Her Christmas would be perfect after all. She'd found real love at last. Peace. A renewed faith. And home. The place she'd been seeking all her life.

And she'd found them because of a tiny baby in a crèche.

Dear Reader,

When our children were growing up, Christmas at our house didn't mean spending lots of money. It did mean having lots of gifts. We learned early on that it didn't matter what the kids got, as long as there were tons of packages to open. Of course, "Santa" always brought what they wanted (or a reasonable facsimile, in case it was a new car), and my husband and I always got them a "big" present. The rest of the gifts were little things: art supplies, books, games, a coveted pocketknife or watch, that special pair of earrings or bottle of perfume.

Our tree, usually cut down in the woods was a happily cluttered tree, laden with a hodge-podge of ornaments. Ornaments we bought out first year of marriage, some from my parents' collection, antique treasures found at the Salvation Army thrift store, things the kids made at school. I even hung a card I received from a friend back in the fourth grade.

Each holiday season we baked cookies of all kinds, including Christmas Cake Cookies (recipe following) to give to friends. Making Christmas cutout cookies, as Carole and the Nicholas kids do in the story, was also a yearly tradition with us.

As the family grew and changed, so did our traditions. It doesn't matter. As long as you're surrounded by family, friends and love, your Christmas is bound to be Merry.

Wishing all my readers a very Merry Christmas and a New Year filled with blessings in abundance.

CHRISTMAS CAKE COOKIES

2 eggs
2 lbs. dates
1 lb. pecans
½ lb. candied cherries (4 oz. red, 4 oz. green)
½ lb. candied pineapple (yellow)
2 ½ cups all-purpose flour
1 ½ cups sugar
1 c. butter (2 sticks)
1 tsp. baking soda
1 tsp. salt
1 tsp cinnamon

Preheat oven to 400° F.

Chop all fruit and nuts. Combine and set aside. Sift together flour, salt, baking soda and cinnamon. Set aside. Cream butter. Add sugar and beat until smooth. Add eggs and beat again. Add flour mixture and stir until dry ingredients are incorporated. Add fruit and nuts. Mix until coated.

Drop mixture from teaspoon onto ungreased cookie sheet. Bake for 10 minutes. Makes 150 - 170 cookies.

ENJOY!!

AN UNTIMELY FROST

Lilly Long Mystery

Book One

Penny Richards

When Shakespearian actress Lilly Long is robbed and abandoned by her new husband, she vows no man will take advantage of her again. Eager to help other women, she uses her acting background to apply for a position with the Pinkertons.

Her first assignment is to find Reverend Harold Purcell and see if he will sell the house he abandoned twenty years earlier. The job sounds easy, but to her surprise the town folk clam up when she mentions his name. When tales of ghosts, theft, seduction and murder begin to surface, she knows this case is about much more than a missing person.

THOUGH THIS BE MADNESS

Lilly Long Mystery

Book Two

Penny Richards

For her second case, Lilly Long and her reluctant partner, Cade McShane are sent to New Orleans to investigate the confinement of a grieving widow into the infamous New Orleans Insane Asylum.

Posing as a married couple doesn't sit well with either of them, but Lilly still has a lot to prove, and Cade needs to redeem himself for past unbecoming behavior.

Little goes on in that the servants don't know about. Set in sultry New Orleans, Lilly and Cade discover lies, affairs, Voodoo and an elaborate scam they never suspected.

Available in bookstores May 2017
Pre-order from your favorite online bookstore

FROM THE AUTHOR

Readers have been asking for it, so I'm pleased to announce the upcoming release of the sixth and final book of the popular "Wolf Creek" series from my new imprint, Penny Pincher Press.

WOLF CREEK WHIMSY
(Win and Ellie's story)

Check out the first chapter:

Wolf Creek, Arkansas, June 1886

The Southwestern Arkansas and Indian Territory Railroad engine ground to a screeching stop, rousing Win Granville from a light sleep. He'd given up on his sleeping berth around midnight. Though he'd mostly been able to stretch out his six-foot-two-inch frame, the narrow sleeping compartment more resembled a coffin than a place of rest.

Hungry and cranky, he'd climbed down from the top berth and found an empty seat near a window, effectively trading one form of misery for another. Thank the Lord they'd finally arrived in Wolf Creek after an exhausting trip to Boston to take care of some business interests he still controlled.

Win sat straighter in his seat, knuckled the gritty feeling from his eyes and peered out the grimy window. It was just daylight. Light shone at the café. Ellie was up, her bread and biscuits already made, getting the popular eating establishment ready for another busy day. His stomach rumbled at the memory of her light-as-a-feather buttermilk biscuits.

A few other business owners were milling around, unlocking doors, flipping signs around from CLOSED to OPEN and sweeping wooden walkways, all in preparation for another day of trade. There was no doubt they were prospering, as much as a business in a town this size could, but he was accustomed to doing business on a larger scale, dealing with enterprises scattered across the country and even a few in Europe. He was used to so much...more.

Another of those unexpected, unaccustomed feelings of self-doubt washed through him. He'd given up a great life and a fantastic yearly income to move to a little town so he could pursue a woman who made it clear every time she crossed his path that she didn't have much use for him. Or at least that's how she acted. There was a part of her though, a part she wasn't so good at hiding, that said without words that he flustered her, and that she was as aware of him as he was her.

His thirty years had been relatively trouble free, but ever since he'd accompanied his mother to the small Arkansas town for a reunion with his step-brothers, Caleb and Gabe Gentry, he hadn't been able to shake the notion that he was drifting through life, never doing anything meaningful or having his will or his intellect tested.

He didn't deny that ever since his beloved

Felicity was killed in a carriage accident on the way to their wedding almost eleven years ago, he'd been more or less content to play the field. As one of the most sought after bachelors in Boston, he'd had his choice of any number of pretty debutantes, none of whom stirred his heart in the slightest.

As he'd grown older, Boston's social scene and his continued toying with women that held no more interest to him than the food on the lavish buffet tables, had lost its appeal. In all those years, he hadn't met a single woman he felt might take Felicity's place in his heart. Until Ellie Carpenter.

And that was the crux of the matter.

He couldn't get the pretty café owner out of his mind. Unsure if that was because he had real feelings for the curvaceous auburn-haired Ellie or because she refused to give him the time of day, Win had convinced himself that he was weary of the sameness of his days and needed a challenge and a change. He'd persuaded himself that moving somewhere else and taking up a different occupation would give his life new meaning. His brother Philip, a highly successful attorney, had told him that this was just another of his whims—of which there had been many through the years—and that this one was likely to be the ruin of him.

He'd done it anyway, and chosen Wolf Creek as the place to start over. So here he was, his whole life turned upside down, all for a woman who claimed she wanted nothing to do with him. He drew in a shaky breath to bolster his spirits and his determination. What was done was done. The bridges leading back to his past life were burned beyond redemption.

The only thing that gave him hope was one bit of good news he'd received while he was in Boston. His sister, Blythe, had sent him a telegram stating that Ellie had confided that she had taken steps to have Jake Carpenter, the husband who had walked out on her the day their daughter was born, declared legally dead. After more than a year of waiting, Ellie was a free woman.

Win wondered why she'd finally decided to put a legal end to her marriage after so many years. Could it possibly mean what he hoped it did? He almost didn't dare to dream that she felt something more for him than she was willing to admit, and every part of him told him that she did feel something for him. He hadn't become one of Boston's most eligible bachelors with his pick of the crème de la crème of debutants without learning all the little "tells" that mean a woman was interested. Whether or not she was ready to admit it, Ellie was not as indifferent to him as she seemed, and whatever her reason for ridding herself of Jake, it was definitely a step in the right direction if, there was ever to be a romantic future for her.

Despite the stalemate in their relationship, his time in Boston had only made him more certain that what he felt for her was real and lasting. He was eager to see her again and gauge for himself if there were any changes in the way she treated him now that she was free, which meant she could no longer use her relationship with Jake to put him, or any other man, off.

Perhaps more importantly, it meant there would be no more pussyfooting around in his pursuit of her. He intended to launch an all-out campaign to win her heart and her love, and he'd use all the skills that had made him a sought-after bachelor for so long, as well as his proficiency in his business dealings.

Win had no doubt that if he put his mind to it, Ellie Carpenter would be his by the end of the year.

Ellie was just filling the coffee cups of her first two patrons of the morning when she glanced out the window and saw the man who had somehow sneaked past the guards she'd erected around her heart, crossing the street. With her insides quivering, she smiled at the two mill bigwigs, told them their breakfast would be right out and headed back toward the kitchen. If only she could stay there, she thought, setting the blue granite coffee pot on the wood-burning stove.

She was considering swapping jobs with her breakfast cook, Gwen, and sending her out to wait tables, when the door swung open and Win stepped into the small café. From her vantage point in the kitchen, she observed his every move through the pass-through, watching him take off his bowler and snag it on the hall tree near the front entrance.

Without even being aware of what she was doing, she picked up the coffeepot once again and moved toward the swinging door that separated the two rooms, her gaze fixed on the man headed toward an empty table near the back. His expression was solemn, but his eyes held a familiar, playful glint, and a smile toyed with the corners of his mouth. "Hello, Ellie. You're looking well."

Always handsome, he nonetheless showed a bit of wear and tear from days of traveling. There were lines of weariness at the corners of his tawny eyes, and his always tidy hair was a bit mussed, as if he'd run his fingers through it. It was apparent that he hadn't shaved, and his lean cheeks were covered with the beginnings of a beard. The slightly scruffy look shouted that even though he was well-turned out and unmistakably citified, he was inarguably all male.

Ellie exhaled a shaky breath. Win was like a box of dynamite. He ought to have a "DANGER" warning stamped on his forehead. "Thank you, Win," she said politely, hoping her smile looked friendly and welcoming. "You're looking..."

Wonderful. Delicious. Amazingly handsome.

"...very well yourself."

He rubbed a palm over his cheek. "I haven't seen a mirror this morning, which is probably a blessing, but it's kind of you to say so."

"I trust your trip back home was a good one."

"My trip was a very good one, but Boston isn't my home anymore. Wolf Creek is."

Before she could reply, he said, "I'm starving. The apple I got from the news butch didn't last very long." As if to put a point on the claim, his stomach gave a loud rumble. "See?" he said with a lift of his eyebrows. "My stomach is asking if my throat's been cut."

Ellie pressed her lips together to keep from smiling. Hearing Big Dan Mercer's favorite down-home saying coming from the mouth of the elegant Granville heir was downright funny, but she resented the fact that he could make her smile over *anything*.

Despite what he said about Wolf Creek being his home, she knew better than to trust his words. Win Granville simply wasn't the type to put down permanent roots in a place with so little to offer. To even think he was serious was a route leading straight to heartbreak. She straightened her shoulders and shored up her backbone.

"I don't suppose you have any of those marvelous biscuits, do you?" he asked.

Determined not to let him charm his way into her heart, she scowled at him. "Don't I always have biscuits?"

"Yes you do, and thank God for it." He pulled out a chair. "Gravy?" he asked with a lift of his brows and a hopeful expression.

If Ellie's smile were any sweeter it would have given him a toothache. "I have an abundance of gravy. Am I to assume you want your regular breakfast?"

Win liked it all. Eggs, biscuits and gravy, whatever breakfast meat took his fancy that day, and grits. To everyone's surprise, he'd taken quite a liking to the southern breakfast staple. He liked the spread served up with fresh-churned butter and blackstrap molasses. Lots of it.

"You are." He actually rubbed his palms together in anticipation. "And lots of coffee, please."

Ellie poured his coffee and left to fix his breakfast. Not sure how much more she could take of Win at the moment, she decided to swap places with Gwen, in order to avoid speaking to him again. At least not today.

Win took a final bite of his biscuits and gravy. Excellent. He looked across the room at Ellie, who had been hiding away in the kitchen but was now taking money from the men who'd come in just before him. She smiled at the customers, and it seemed that the room got brighter. His heart seemed to stumble before it picked up a ragged rhythm. At that moment, she looked over and their gazes clashed. Even from where he sat, he could tell she was blushing.

Because he knew she'd come to expect something outrageous from him, he winked at her. She lifted her chin and turned away. He smiled, his spirits suddenly buoyed. He'd been challenged before and everything had turned out okay. Ellie Carpenter had no idea how her life was about to change.

Deliberately turning away from the dratted man who managed to fluster her despite her efforts not to let him, Ellie escaped once more to the anonymity of the kitchen.

"Are you all right?"

Gwen, her waitress and fill-in cook, was

looking at her with a furrowed brow.

"Fine," Ellie managed with remarkable nonchalance considering that blood was still racing through her veins at an alarming speed. "Why?"

"You just look sort of flushed."

"It's summertime. It's hot," she said, as if that settled the matter.

"Are you sure Win Granville doesn't have something to do with it?" Gwen asked.

"Don't be ridiculous," Ellie snapped, stirring a bit of water into the milk gravy that sat warming...and thickening...at the back of the wood stove.

Gwen broke two eggs into the hot bacon grease and laughed. "That man has feelings for you, and if you don't feel something for him, maybe you ought to have Doc Rachel check to make sure you still have a pulse."

Oh, she had a pulse all right. And at the moment, it was beating crazily fast. "Don't be ridiculous," she said again. Then added, "Are those eggs about ready?"

"In a jiffy," Gwen told her.

Win lingered over his coffee, enjoying the home cooking and watching Ellie as she flitted back and forth from the kitchen to the dining room and from table to table. In her pale yellow gingham dress, she reminded him of a honeybee flitting from flower to flower.

He tried to imagine her in the house he'd purchased from Nate Haversham, the previous banker, a few months ago. With the help of his mother and his sister, he been making some changes in the colors and furnishings, and while those changes more matched his style, the place still didn't feel like home. It would take something more to do that. Or someone. Someone like Ellie with her bright smile and her kind heart and her infectious laughter ... whenever she loosened up enough to allow herself to laugh.

As if his thinking about it made it happen, he heard the sound of her laughter echo throughout the room. She was standing near the table of a couple of farmers who'd come in from their fields, probably to pick up something from Gabe Gentry at the mercantile, and decided to splurge on a bought breakfast before loading up and heading back home. Giving them a smile, she turned and headed toward his table to refill his coffee cup.

"Is everything okay?" she asked, reaching out with the large speckled coffee pot and pouring his cup to the top.

"Not really."

She looked as if he'd struck her, especially considering that his plate was empty. "What is it? The ham? Were the eggs not cooked right?"

"Settle down, Ellie," he said, reaching out to catch hold of her free hand.

When his thumb began to make slow concentric circles on the back of her hand, her gaze found his and she tried to pull free. "What are you doing?"

"Trying to get you to talk to me just once without being so prickly and standoffish." His voice was soft, even cajoling, but there was just the slightest bit of steel in it that said he would be heard.

She sucked in a breath of surprise. "I'm not."

"Oh, yes you are."

"What does that have to do with your breakfast?"

"Nothing."

Her smooth forehead puckered in a frown. "But you said..."

"I know what I said. Everything won't be okay with me until you admit that you're as attracted to me as I am to you."

She grew as still as a deer who scented a hunter nearby. "I'm not." Her voice was breathless, but held no firmness.

"Liar."

"I'm not lying."

"Your pulse says you are."

"Stop it, Win!"

She hissed the words in a low whisper. This time the jerk she gave her hand freed her from his hold. Without another word, she turned and almost stomped to the kitchen, pushing the swinging saloon-type door so hard, it whacked the wall.

Scooting back his chair and standing, Win tossed his napkin to the tabletop, and followed her, not caring a whit that people were staring at him.

When he got to the big cast iron stove, Gwen was stepping aside so that Ellie could take her place. She glanced at Win with a shrug and a smile before heading out with the coffeepot to take care of the breakfast customers.

Only when he was alone with Ellie did he ask, "Stop what?"

She flung a narrow-eyed gaze over her shoulder. "Ooh!" she said so vehemently that he fully expected her to stamp her foot. "You know exactly what I mean. Stop flirting with me. We both know you mean nothing by it, and all it does is make me...make me..."

"Make you what?"

"Make me mad!"

"Why on earth would it make you mad? You're a beautiful, sweet, godly woman. And I hear you're available," he tacked on when she cast him another furious look. "And I'm a man who appreciates those qualities."

"So I've heard." She picked up some ham with a two-pronged fork and placed it on a platter before cracking two eggs into the hot fat. "In fact I've heard from your sister that back in Boston you went through available women like you changed your socks."

"This isn't Boston."

"It certainly isn't."

"You're not like any of those women."

She laughed then, a little sound that held a self-deprecatory note. "I most certainly am not, and that, I'm sure you will agree, is the heart of the problem."

Win, who was thoroughly enjoying seeing this feisty, testy side of her, plunged his hands into the pockets of his rumpled navy pinstripe suit and leaned back against the doorframe as if he hadn't a care in the world. Inside, his own stomach was tied into a knot that threatened to choke him. "What problem?"

"Don't play thickheaded with me, Winston Granville. You know what I mean. You're a big city boy. I'm a country girl."

"That's true," he said with a slow nod. "And?"

"You're well-educated. College educated. I'm not."

"You're as sharp as a tack."

"Stop making light of this, Win!" she cried, and this time she did stamp her foot. "I'm being serious."

"Yes, you are. Too serious. But I must say that nothing you've said so far carries any weight that I can see. Haven't you ever heard about opposites attracting?"

"Who said I'm attracted to you?"

He gave an elegant lift of his shoulders. "Maybe because there would be no need for you to point out all the reasons things wouldn't work between us if you aren't."

Knowing he had her, she just shook her head and placed a couple of biscuits on the edge of the plate she was preparing, and continued to baste the eggs with the grease.

Gwen came back into the kitchen. "Waymon's eggs about ready?"

"Just about," Ellie said. Only after she'd added the soft fried eggs to the plate and Gwen scooped it up and carried out of the room did Ellie say anything to Win.

When she turned to look at him, her eyes were glazed with tears. A stab of guilt pierced his heart for causing her any grief. Then he reminded himself of what his father had always said: Faint heart never won fair lady...or something like that.

She pushed a stray lock of reddish-brown hair away from her flushed face with the back of her hand. "What do you want from me, Win?"

"Why did you finally have Jake declared dead?" he asked, without answering.

It was her time to shrug. "Everyone kept telling me I should, and it made sense...the timing just seemed...right, somehow."

"Why, Ellie?" he pressed. "You're not the only one who hears gossip. I've heard there have been a lot of men who wanted to court you, and you wouldn't give them the time of day because you said you were too uncertain where you stood with your marriage. So I'm asking again. Why see to it that you're free now, after thirteen years?"

She turned away. Win straightened and went to her, placing his hands on her shoulders. She tried to shrug free. Instead of releasing her, he forced her to turn and face him. His heart was pounding in his chest as he placed his fist beneath her chin and lifted it, demanding that she look at him.

"What do you want me to say, Win?"

"I want you to say yes."

Confusion clouded her eyes. "Yes? Yes to what? Yes, I'll agree to see you socially?"

"No. I want to take care of you forever, Ellie Carpenter. I want to give you things and make you happy. I want us to be a family."

He saw understanding in her widening eyes.
"I want to marry you, Ellie Carpenter. Say yes."

Forbidden

by LaRee Bryant

Ecuador, 1899

Headstrong, rich, and beautiful, Jordan St. Clair is determined to find her fiancé and break her engagement even if it means an ocean voyage and a trek into the dangerous wilds of the Amazon jungle. After all, she's hired the top guide in the country.

Stunned to find out his new employer is a woman but desperate to save his reputation and his mortgaged-to-the-hilt farm, Patrick Castle swallows his irritation and his pride and grudgingly agrees to break his rule of no women on expedition. His one hope is that the all too real dangers of the jungle will quickly scare Jordan into calling off her quest.

Far too stubborn to back down even if it means they might wind up in real danger of losing their lives, neither realizes that their hearts are in even greater jeopardy.

MURDER, HE HOWLED

Sandy Steen

Gifted with looks and money, Parker Doyle is a real catch, right? There's just one problem. He's a best-selling author, a college professor and, oh yeah, a Werewolf. Now, don't panic--he's not *that* kind of Werewolf. In fact, he locks himself up at every full moon, so how bad can he be?

When people connected to Parker start turning up dead, he fears he's being framed. Now he's forced to use his curse to solve the crimes. Throw in a sexy stalker, a deranged fan and a sweet-natured animal lover fascinated with wolves . . . and things get really hairy.